# The Ingredients of Gumbo

Every family is a unique stew of personalities, memories and shared events. When stirred with care and respect, the mix produces a lifetime's feast of love.

Julia Schuster's stories about Southern families—their dreams, feuds and peculiarities reflect the universal appeal of all families everywhere—the rich, deep and fulfilling bond of tolerant affection.

*"I watch the members of my family file into the dining room, one by one, ingredients, each of them, yes, a menagerie of peculiar ingredients that make no sense at all together until they are thrown into the pot and simmered for a while."*

*The Ingredients of Gumbo* treats readers to an artful mix of stories, poems, recipes and gentle, sassy opinion, mingling the exotic and familiar, the funny and sad—all the intricate flavors, textures and spices of life in the South. Julia explores it all—the complex and often comical relationships in families, her unwavering faith, the shared bond of food, and her discovery of the joy found in reaching outside her family—indeed, across the globe—to help others.

Sit back, grab a glass of sweet tea and enjoy!

*To Sissie*

# The Ingredients of Gumbo

*Stories, poems, sassy opinions & sketches served with love.*
*Mix well & savor. Good to the last hug!*

*by*

## *Julia Schuster*

Bell Bridge Books

# The Ingredients of Gumbo

ISBN: 978-1-61194-007-7

This is a work of fiction. Names, characters, places and incidents are either the products of the author's imagination or are used fictitiously. Any resemblance to actual persons (living or dead,) events or locations is entirely coincidental.

Bell Bridge Books
PO BOX 300921
Memphis, TN 38130
Bell Bridge Books is an Imprint of BelleBooks, Inc.

Printed and bound in the United States of America.

We at BelleBooks enjoy hearing from readers.

Visit our websites – www.BelleBooks.com and www.BellBridgeBooks.com.

10 9 8 7 6 5 4 3 2

Cover design: Debra Dixon
Interior design: Martha Crockett
Interior art:  Julia Schuster
Backgrounds (manipulated) © Sashsmir | Dreamstime.com
Utensils (manipulated) © Michael Higginson | Dreamstime.com

## A note from the author—

*The Ingredients of Gumbo* is a collection of my fiction, nonfiction, poetry, recipes, opinion and art. The selections were written over a ten-year period and were specifically chosen to illustrate the evolutionary process of growing up, living and being Southern.

The people you'll read about—both the flesh-n-blood varieties and the fictional ones that exist only in my head—are the unexpected and blessed ingredients that have spiced the recipe of my life. They may not make much sense when scattered about in stories, but when mixed together just so and allowed to simmer awhile, their richness melds and marries the life experiences of the most divine recipe in the universe: my life.

—Julia

I am a little pencil in the
hand of God, who is writing a
love letter to the world.

—Mother Teresa

# *My Boring Life*

I often write stories about my sister. And it always drives her nuts. I'm sure it is because I never fail to mention that she is my older sister, my much, much older sister by thirteen long, gray and wrinkled years. The fact that she gives me such a ready supply of hysterical anecdotes doesn't help her situation. She is constantly hot under her underwires because of my latest newspaper column outlining her unnatural fears— like her paranoia about the varmints that live in the woods behind her house, or the skink (that's a lizard) that lives in her garage and delivers mysterious globs of black and white polka-dot poop all over her boxed-up keepsakes. Then there is her unending search for the perfect carrot cake; not any recipe will do. It has to be just so-so, moist without being spongy; with cream cheese icing that is sweet without making her lips pucker distastefully like grocery store birthday cakes. A sister like mine is a celestial gift to a writer whose life has been as unremarkably boring as mine.

So, when she dared me to write about myself, dared me to regurgitate something, anything that I had done that might shine the proverbial spotlight on me for a change, I could hardly refuse. She is my sister, after all. I would do anything for her, even if she didn't live close enough to convince her skink friend to move to my house if I didn't cooperate.

She leaned over my shoulder one day. I stared blankly at my computer screen, wondering what I would write about her next. The miniature reflection in my screen of her face glowing back at me gave me a chill. The blue haze reflected in her glasses gave her eyes an ethereal gleam. Her arms reached over my shoulders and gently lifted my hands from my lap, placing my fingers ceremoniously on the keys. Then those same hands gripped my shoulders. Her breathy words, husky in my ears, said, "This time you will write something about yourself." The pressure of her cheek against the side of my head let me know that this wasn't a simple suggestion, but instead, an order I had no choice but to accept.

My next quandary was: What can I possibly write about my life?

Sissie had some ideas to get me going, of course. "What about the time . . ." started the next fifteen sentences out of her mouth, each weighted by an authority only an elder sister can pull off. She astonished me with her memory for the less than flattering episodes in my life. Her recitation of ideas complete, she commanded, "Type! I expect ten pages resembling some version of truth before this day calls it quits."

She strode out of my office, leaving me to fester, ponder and procrastinate alone. Finally, slowly, my fingers twitched, then wiggled. I held my breath and let it flow.

I stood in the living room of our singlewide, a shotgun loaded with birdshot in my hands. My husband paced the untreated wooden deck that hung precariously off the backside of our listing house. Screaming loud enough to be heard three doublewides away, I yelled, "Marv Jackson, I swear I'll blow you off this world if I even think you've been running around on me again." To make my point, I lifted the barrel to chest level and pulled one trigger. The sliding glass doors took the brunt of the blast. My clueless husband took flight and took cover. Marv Jackson vaulted the deck rails just in the nick of time to save his neck.

"Holy Cowhide," he hollered from his crouched position under the deck. He knew better than to lift his head above the deck flooring. I still had another barrel yet to discharge. "You could have killed me. You're crazy, woman! And you wonder why I look elsewhere every now and then."

Needless to say, the last blast whizzed a little too close to his backside for comfort. I'm sure that, if the trailer has survived all these years in tornado alley, the holes in the deck boards remain there to this day.

I sat back, not believing what I had just written. *Oh, my Lord*, my mind screeched. *I used to be poor white trash!* I hadn't realized it before. I used to live in a house trailer and threatened my sorry, good-for-nothing husband with bodily harm on a regular basis. How could this be? Do I know this woman? Could that have really been me?

Sissie must have sensed my personal turmoil. Her presence shadowed me again, accompanied by the distinct aroma of pure cane sugar and nutmeg. The grip on my shoulders was more

You can kid the world, but not a sister.
—Charlotte Gray

comforting somehow, floury and maternal, but no less determined. "It was you," she said with a satisfied grin, "Or some fictional version of yourself. Who knows? Who cares? The point is: You can tell a good tale, so get to it."

Some strangled adaptation of that scene had happened years and years ago, of course. I did vaguely remember my ex-husband owning a shotgun, and cardboard doors and masking tape had replaced broken glass sliders, hadn't they? The hussy who'd slept with my husband right there in our love nest on wheels was as vivid in my memory as the face of my first dog, wasn't she? Oh, and the Naugahide couch that took up half the room and could hide a case of empty beer cans between its cushions without getting lumpy will forever remain fresh. It often swallowed friends and family members when they made the mistake of passing out within its reach. (The hussy held similar qualities, as I recall.)

Sissie was not done with me yet, not by a long shot. She rattled off a few other choice story possibilities. "What about how your marriage got started in the first place? Remember that . . .?"

"Oh, no, but I was just a child, an innocent child," I stuttered. "You can't hold that one mistake against me. I wasn't old enough to know any better. Come on, Sissie, gimme a break."

"A determined little cus' and a spoiled brat is more like it," she said. "Go on, write the story. It'll be good for you. Write!"

I met Mother in the Goldsmith's Department Store Bridal Department one afternoon in November of 1974. I knew I was supposed to try on wedding dresses that day, but for some unknown reason, it had not occurred to me that a bra might be required to make the bodice fit right. Mother almost fell out in the floor when I dropped my raggedy hip-huggers, revealing black satin, Saturday Night bikini panties. The suggestive red lettering left little to the imagination. The bridal consultant excused herself, while Mother blessed me out and then struggled to compose what was left of her "last nerve." There I stood, bare-chested, in my streetwalker panties and multi-colored knee socks with each toe nestled snugly in its own little knitted sweater. I wiggled my toes.

Mother wept.

A few weeks later, Daddy drove as Mother bawled beside him in the front seat. I can still hear her sniffling. She waved Granny's tear-soaked, hand-embroidered hanky like a white flag, wishing for clemency, wishing for the miracle of my father saying, "NO," to me for the first time in my life.

Marv Jackson and I sat quietly behind them. I was every day of seventeen. Marv Jackson was three years older, old enough to know better. I stared at him with all the adoration of a toddler gazing at a beagle pup. All of my friends and family thought I was pregnant—what other reason could there be for my determination to get married so quickly?—but I fooled them; I was marrying for love!

Mother cried so loudly as Daddy signed the "consent for underage marriage" papers, I thought the County Clerk was going to have to ask her to leave.

My hands shook compulsively. I could hardly keep them on the keys. I was glad Sissie had disappeared into the other room. The realizations that now flooded over me could not be a pretty sight to watch. Had I blocked out my whole life? Had I selectively filed away the distasteful memories of my young adulthood, choosing to focus on the major flub-ups of others to keep from having to stare wide-eyed at the crazed beast looking back at me in the mirror? Naw, couldn't be. I am a writer. Spinning tales is what I do. But now, I couldn't stop myself. More bile rose in the back of my throat, determined to come up and out.

His souped-up red Camaro was parked out front. I had been planning to surprise him all week with news of the sale of our house in Little Rock. Now we could be together again, after so many months apart. A red-orange glow enveloped the new apartment complex. *He'll be so glad to see me,* I thought. *This will be a night better than the honeymoon we never had.* I rapped hard on the door, unbuttoned an extra button on my shirt and took up my best super model slouch, biting my lips to give them voluptuous color.

The door creaked open, and my best friend, Lucille, greeted me with a strangled expression of disbelief.

"Marv Jackson," she called over her shoulder, "I think you should come here. We've got company."

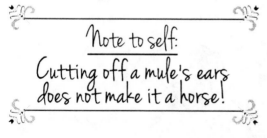

I glanced down at Lucille's roundness. I hadn't seen her in several months with all the hubbub of preparing to move and all. Now, I noticed that she seemed to have gained a great deal of weight. When she turned sideways to wrap her arms around the neck of my husband, I realized that it was a pregnant tummy that protruded from her midsection, not added on pounds from one too many visits to the Dairy Queen.

"What are you doing here?" Marv Jackson hollered.

( Is it just me, or has my life been played out in louder than normal tones?)

"We sold the house, honey," I chimed. "I came to tell you. Lucille, good

to see you. What are you doing here?" I guess it was shock from being slapped in the face by reality, but for some reason my senses had taken a hike and all I could do was stand there like a frozen cucumber, staring at the big belly of my best friend. We had gone to high school together. She had met Marv Jackson at a football game, dated him, discarded him and introduced him to me. I had accepted her leftovers with open arms. Our relationship had been off and on since my marriage to her off-cast, but I had still considered her my dearest friend.

"Well, I guess it is high time you found out," she said, slapping me again and back to the present. "Marv Jackson and I are in love. We're having a baby and, as soon as you are out of the picture, we are getting married and will live happily ever after."

Marv Jackson moved a little closer in behind her, taking cover. His eyes darted around nervously, making sure I didn't pull a shotgun from my macramé handbag.

Sometime later, I'm not sure how long, days maybe, weeks, certainly hours, my nose reacted to an incoming aroma. It filled my home office with the scent of cinnamon, vanilla and cream. I moved toward the kitchen, curious as to what Sissie had been doing while I threw up tidbits of my actual and fictional past. She welcomed me to my own kitchen with a sugary hug.

"Ready for some carrot cake, Lovebug?" she asked, wiping a stray tear from my cheek. "I think I've finally discovered the secret to carrot cake. Now if I can just remember exactly what I did to make this confectionery masterpiece."

I dipped my finger into her bowl of cream cheese icing and brought it to my lips. They did not pucker. The creaminess slid onto my tongue like a velvet gift.

"The cake springs back, but it's not bouncy," she said, beaming. "Meet perfection—the perfect carrot cake and the perfect sister team."

"We are a team," I managed. My throat tightened. I realized that moment that my sister was the closest thing to perfect I'd ever known. I couldn't speak. All I could do was hug her neck and weep.

# Sissie's Carrot Cake

2 cups all purpose flour
2 tsp. baking soda
½ tsp. salt
2 tsp. cinnamon
3 eggs
2 cups sugar
¾ cup vegetable oil
¾ cup buttermilk
2 tsp. vanilla
2 cups grated carrot
1 can crushed pineapple, drained
1 can coconut
1½ cup chopped pecans

Grease and flour 3 round cake pans. Stir together first four ingredients.
Beat eggs and next 4 ingredients until smooth. Add flour mixture until smooth.
Stir in carrots and next 3 ingredients.

Bake 350 degrees for 25-30 minutes. When cool, ice with cream cheese icing.

# Cream Cheese Icing

¾ Cup soft butter
1½ pkg. cream cheese (12 ounces)
2 boxes powdered sugar
1 tsp. lemon juice
1 tsp. vanilla

Cream together until smooth.

# Author's Note

Lord knows I hope my writing has improved since those first feeble attempts at storytelling. And that my choices in characters and situation have matured. This collection is made up of a few of my efforts. Some are fiction, others nonfiction, and then there are the selections that are a combination of both. Only I know the ingredients that mixed together to make the whole. I'll never divulge my "literary recipe," but I hope you will have fun guessing what I mixed together and how.

Happy Reading!

# The Ingredients of Gumbo

*(Awarded 1ˢᵗ Place in Fiction, Metroversity Literary Competition, Louisville, KY, 2007)*

I had never thought much about gumbo until Christmas eight years ago, although it had always been a part of my at-least-once-a-month cuisine. Ah, that Christmas. The memory of it is as clear to me as a Waterford crystal vase. Mother always served gumbo for Christmas Eve lunch, with an assortment of my other favorite Creole or Cajun recipes. Gumbo is a family tradition, chock full of sausage and duck, fresh rabbit and venison, or my favorite crawfish and shrimp, depending on Mother's mood and what Daddy drags in from his latest hunting trip. Even an occasional snake shows up in the rich, dark roux, all displayed on Mother's finest china, of course.

Now, sitting in my usual spot just to the right of Mother's place, I watch the members of my family file into the dining room, one by one. Ingredients, each of them. Yes, a menagerie of peculiar ingredients that make no sense at all together until they are thrown into the pot and simmered for awhile. But memories of that Christmas Eve prevent me from enjoying the beginnings of this one and transport me back to a Christmas Eve when I glanced across the dining room table at my bug-eyed Yankee cousin, Mimzie. It was that Christmas Eve when my thoughts on gumbo and our other fine Louisiana delicacies were transformed.

Everyone had just settled into their seats, linen napkins smoothed across Sunday bested laps, polite sips of water taken, heads bowed, chests crossed in the name of the Trinity, grace spoken aloud and in unison, when Mother lifted the lid off her Villeroy and Bach hand-painted soup tureen to reveal its contents. It was then that Mimzie's prim face contorted into that of the spoiled child her adolescence struggled but failed to disguise.

"I will not consume amphibians, Thumper, ocean creatures, or any kind of sausage," she declared. "There is no way to know what horrid things they put in that stuff. And boo-dine sounds absolutely disgusting. How can you put that in your mouths?"

"Boudin" was what Mimzie mistakenly spoke ill of—the tastiest sausage known to man, if you ask me. And certainly, I did know exactly what Mother stuffed into her hog casings—Great-Grandma Vermaelen's secret recipe of the finest mixture of rice, spices and pork parts in Rapides Parish—that's what. Heck, the finest anywhere east of Shreveport, if you ask me again.

Mimzie pushed her plate a little too forcefully away. Then she didn't even react as the gold edge of my mother's wedding china soup bowl clinked against the delicate stem of my great-grandmother's (on my father's side) water goblet. The stem snapped at the point of injury. Its goblet toppled, dowsing Grandma Vermaelen's crocheted tablecloth with pink lemonade. Conversation came to an almost deafening halt as the tulip shaped globe rolled across the table, leaving its stem in place beside Mimzie's plate. The globe came to rest next to the platter of cornbread at the table's heart. Thank the Good Lord Grandma Menard's sugar bowl survived unscathed.

Mimzie wadded up her napkin, one of a set of twelve that had been handed down to my mother by the matriarch of the Longchamp family some twenty-five years ago, and tossed it into the place her plate once held. She crossed her arms over her barely-blossoming breast with a "humph" and a long sigh.

I could hardly believe my eyes or my ears. No adult had yet uttered a word. I sat there, awe struck. My head would have been the next thing rolling across the table, if I had tried to pull off that kind of stunt. I wondered how on God's green earth this Yankee stuck-up could get away with manners like these. I knew things were different in New York City, but "manners are manners no matter where you are," Mother always said.

And I had never dared to disagree—until now. I tried to justify my dumb cousin's behavior, but to no avail. After all, this was the girl who had traveled about-as-far-South-as-you-can-get for Christmas, wearing a full-length wool coat and expecting to need it. She must not have a brain in her head. Suddenly, I realized that my spoon was still suspended in mid-air not two inches outside of my mouth. I eased it back into my bowl, careful not to make a sound that might turn all eyes toward me.

My mother dabbed politely with her napkin at the little parentheses around her mouth. "Sister, don't you have anything constructive to say to *your* child?" she asked Auntie Jeanne. She folded her napkin neatly and placed it back into her lap. "And you might consider doing it *before* lemonade dribbles off the table and into the laps of my guests." She cut her eyes toward Auntie Jeanne who sat to her left, her polite smile never wavering.

Auntie's face flushed, but not from embarrassment; it was anger that rose scarlet from the "V" of her Fifth Avenue business suit. Her knuckles whitened around the handle of the 100-year-old silver knife she had just used to butter her cornbread. When the butt of it and her fist met the table, every goblet on the table shuddered. Eight iced teas quaked. A few even lost their lemons, which fell, *kerplop*, into the icy depths of their sweetened amber liquid.

"No," Auntie Jeanne growled through her teeth, "I do not have anything to say to *my* daughter. I am not about to force-feed her road kill like Mama and Daddy did to me."

I glanced around the table, keeping my head low and out of the line of Mother's sights. Uncle Jed, Mother and Auntie Jeanne's brother, looked up at me and grinned a big toothy grin. I smiled back. He reminded me of a kindly Jed Clampett, only with the mental capacity of a decidedly more dimwitted Jethro. Some said he was mentally retarded, but I didn't believe it. I had always just thought of him as a tad-bit slow. He and his rotund wife, Ethel, now stared at their plates.

Mimzie glared across the table at me, as if daring me to open my mouth and stick my foot into deep doggy-doo. I just rolled my eyes at her. Daddy, sitting at the far end of our football field and well out of Mother's range, chugged long on his red wine. He smirked at the commotion as if enjoying the possibility of another family free-for-all. Mimzie, still pouting, then had the gall to bring her shoeless foot up and place it in the chair seat with her buttocks. She hugged her knee. At this, it took great effort to keep my jaw from going slack.

"I don't seem to recall any force-feeding from our childhood, but that's not the point," Mother said, leveling her gaze on her own plate. Her fingers now traced little curly-ques in the perspiration on her goblet. "I think there is something to be said for proper upbringing in the social arts, Sister, and your dear, darlin' Mimzie seems to have no recollection of hers."

"I have proper social arts," Mimzie whined, daring again. "But I'm still not eating this creepy, crawly crap."

I inhaled so fast and so deeply I almost choked on the air. This girl had balls, as Daddy would say. I wasn't sure what that meant at the time, but it seemed appropriate in this case. For the puny little so-and-so she appeared to be, Mimzie was either the bravest person I had ever met or the most likely to die without knowing how butt-dumb she really was.

Mother turned her head only slightly in the direction of the latest transgression. Her kind eyes fell upon Mimzie's obstinate face. Her voice, soft and low, caressed the air. "Mimzie dear, I know your long trip from the North must have been difficult and tiring. I understand the trials of shuffling luggage from here to there, and deciphering airline hieroglyphics with all their abbreviations, schedules and such. But I had so hoped that this would be a pleasant family meal, devoid of hysterics and rudeness. It is our custom here in Louisiana to celebrate this special holiday with hospitality, courtesy and a good helping of respect for our place in life. You understand what I mean, I'm sure."

Mimzie glanced over at her mother, who looked like she was about to oxidize. Then she glared back at my mother who was still rattling on.

"In light of that, my dear, I would certainly appreciate it if you would kindly place the soles of your shoeless feet back on the Oriental rug beneath your chair, sit up straight so no one will mistake you for a pack mule, pick up your spoon like the civilized human being you have no other choice but to be, and eat something, anything that I have slaved in my hot kitchen to prepare."

I said a silent *Hail Mary* when Mimzie did as she was told. The rest of the meal was consumed in the silence that follows a fallen tree. Everyone knew that, after Mother had had her say, no other sentiments mattered.

I knew better than to cause a ruckus about sharing my bedroom with Mimzie. I just led her upstairs after dinner and pointed to the

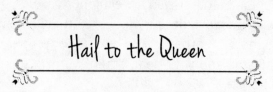

## Hail to the Queen

lumpier sibling of my twin bed. No one, other than Grandma Menard, had ever slept in it. When I had girlfriends come over for slumber parties, we always took over the den downstairs, preferring distance from my parents. Mimzie tossed her carry-on bag onto the bed, then followed suit with herself. She belly-flopped into the middle of the mattress and burrowed her face deep into the pink and lime green plaid taffeta pillow shams.

"Lofff stuuuuuns," she muttered into the old down.

"What?" I asked, unable to decipher the muffled words.

"Loffff Stuuuuuuns," she said again, but I still didn't catch it.

"One more time?" I asked, and wondered how I'd survive a whole month of this brat.

She lifted her head for an instant, and screeched, "Life Stinks!" Then buried it once again.

I plopped down on the edge of my bed and stifled the urge to reply, "Maybe yours, but not mine." Really, I knew very little about this foreigner. Sure, we were related by blood, but she grew up above the Mason-Dixon Line, which made her an alien to me. I knew nothing about her life, except what I had deduced from her behavior at dinner. And I wasn't so sure I wanted to know more. I decided I had better just be polite. After all, she was going to be here at least another month, well past the first of the year, or so I'd been told.

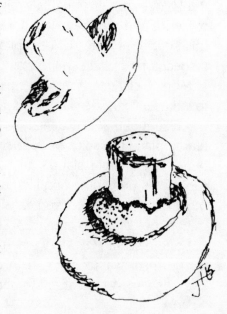

Mother's warnings that, "If you can't say something nice, don't say anything at all," echoed in my ears. But I couldn't just sit there and say nothing. I had learned from example that fake nice works when you're in a pinch. I decided to give it a try.

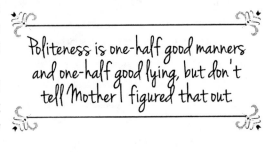

*Politeness is one-half good manners and one-half good lying, but don't tell Mother I figured that out.*

"Long trip, huh?" I managed. "Traveling all that way must be tough, especially with the holiday rush."

Mimzie slowly rolled over onto her back and sat up, staring at me like I'd said, "Buggers, beans and bug's eyes. Would you like some for lunch?"

"The trip has nothing to do with anything, Aza Claire," she huffed. "What is it with Southerners? You think getting on a plane ruins your life. That witch you call a mother made it sound like my manners, or lack of them, were okay somehow because I had flown on a plane." She paused, as if realizing suddenly that she was almost screaming. She reached back and fluffed up her pillows, then leaned back into them and spoke again in a calmer tone. "No, my life stinks because I am a part of this family. You'd think yours smells too, if you had any sense."

I had to ponder this statement for a moment. I realized that she probably thought I was taking so much time to answer because all Southerners are slow, but I was really stumped and didn't want to rush into a reply. I had always thought of my family as being a little eccentric, but all the members I had ever met—until today—were pleasant, friendly, polite, civil and only explosive when something big got in their way. Either Mimzie knew family members I had never met, or she was mistaking our family for some other clan. I lay back, twirling my auburn pigtail around my finger and dangling my legs off the bed. I stared at the ceiling, so I didn't have to see her reaction to what I was about to say. I was almost a year older than her, after all, which meant I didn't have to care what she thought. Age rules.

"Well," I began, "I don't know who all you've met. There are hundreds of us, you know, if you count all the first, second, third and beyond cousins, those related by blood or those who just like us and claim us as kin. But I know most of them, and I have to say that they all seem pretty regular to me—all except *you*, of course."

I brought my head up and rested it on crossed arms behind my head so I could keep an eye on her. I was ready to hold my breath to avoid the A-bomb mushroom, or to protect myself with pillows and kicking feet if it came to that, but I didn't get the chance. A loud commotion startled us both. Battle cries coming from downstairs or outside somewhere caused us to sit up straight, grab our chests and gasp.

"What the heck was that?" I asked aloud without expecting an answer. I came to my feet. Mimzie must have recognized the howls because she was already standing and headed toward the door. I caught up with her at the top of the stairs. Then, a gunshot stopped us both in our tracks, teetering on the top step. Mimzie grabbed my hand, her eyes wild with fear. Without thinking, we thundered halfway down the steps, then slowed to a creep, realizing simultaneously that flying into danger might not be such a good idea.

At the bottom of the steps I peered around the entry hall doorframe into the formal living room. No one was there. I turned silently, moving under the staircase toward the back of the house. I tried to motion for Mimzie to follow, but realized that she was still gripping my hand. My breath felt ragged. My heart thumped so loudly in my ears it almost drowned out my reeling thoughts.

The kitchen stood empty, dinner dishes still stacked on the cabinets, the dishwasher open, but not filled. Muffled noises coming from the back porch drew us forward. We tiptoed across the linoleum. I turned the crystal doorknob of the back door and eased it open. The screen door moaned as I pushed against it. We closed it silently behind us and stepped out onto the porch.

"How could you, Jed? Ethel, can't you control your husband? That tree limb could have been one of us!" Mother griped, struggling to get back to her feet from a crouched position. Finally, she stood erect on the lawn behind Uncle Jed's truck. Her favorite lemonade pitcher and matching glasses were strewn about her, broken into fine pieces of pink crystal. The warm December air quickly melted the ice cubes and the liquid seeped into the grass at her feet. She pointed with her now empty metal serving tray toward Uncle Jed. "You could have killed somebody. Just look at what a mess."

Uncle Jed stood, obviously paralyzed by his own actions, staring at the destruction before him. Daddy's shotgun dangled from his hands and his face muscles lay slack against his cheekbones. A large limb from the ancient oak tree that had stood in our back yard since nineteen-ought-one now protruded from the windshield of Jed's red Toyota truck. The hood of the vehicle had buckled from the force and weight of the limb. The right headlight, popped out like a gouged eyeball, swayed back and forth, suspended from its electrical wires.

Aunt Ethel emerged from her ducking-spot behind a gardenia bush and threw her hands into the air. "Hush. Do you hear me?" she screeched at my mother. "Just hush, Miss High and Mighty. I've heard just about enough out of you for one day. And I can't take anymore." Her fists dug into her waist as she strutted across the lawn,

*Old Chinese Proverb:*
*All people are your relatives,*
*therefore expect only trouble of them.*

headed toward Mother. I stared in amazement. I had never heard this woman speak above a whisper, not to mention with her head upright and eye-to-eye. Uncle Jed usually did all the talking, nonsense mostly, in his usual jovial manner. But now, it was obvious by his stunned expression, he was too overcome to have much to say.

Auntie Jeanne appeared from behind the dormant azaleas where she had taken cover, and headed toward Uncle Jed. "It's okay, Brother," she reassured him. "Just give me the gun. It's all right, now. It's only a truck."

Daddy sat, relaxed in his favorite rocker on the porch to our left with his feet propped up on the rail. He puffed on his cigar, unfazed, and then spit tiny bits of tobacco over the rail through his teeth. Mimzie still gripped my hand so tightly circulation was becoming difficult. I shook her loose. "It's over. Everybody's still alive. But Uncle Jed's truck might not survive," I said. Her peachy complexion had turned a vacant gray.

My red faced Aunt Ethel stomped up to Mother and stopped not six inches from her face. "You're the one who ruined dinner," she yelled. "Bitch, bitch, bitch, all you do is bitch. It is no wonder those girls are so clueless. You lie to their faces every day of their lives, then expect them to act like prissy little ladies to suit your own deluded hopes and dreams." She cut her eyes toward Auntie Jeanne who was still tending to Uncle Jed. "Leave him alone. He is my husband. Don't touch him. You've done enough to screw up his life. Lord knows, having the two of you for sisters has ruined him. The poor love has a heart of gold and a conscience so riddled with guilt he can hardly tie his shoes without coming unglued."

At this, Daddy sat forward in his chair and leaned his elbows on the railing, his eyes now intent on what was unfolding in the yard.

"Well, I never," Mother stuttered. She brushed off her skirt from where she had hit the dirt when the shooting began, winced, and looked down at her hands, then picked at her palms like slivers of broken crystal might be imbedded there. "We have done no such-a thing," she grumbled in a pouty way I'd never known her to use. "He is our brother. We love him. You make it sound like we have hurt him in some way." She glanced up into Aunt Ethel's eyes, but not with anger. She had brought out her mousy Southern charm to defuse the situation with politeness and to avoid bloodshed. "We've always done our best to make sure his life was safe and secure, that he didn't have to deal with all the trials and tribulations of life."

"Dog doody! That's just smelly old dog doody!" Aunt Ethel replied. She waved her hands in Mother's face, which contorted from sweet Southern lady into rabid dog in an instant.

"Oh, get over it—both of you," Auntie Jeanne growled from her place next to Uncle Jed. He still hadn't given up his weapon, so she reached over and snatched it. He didn't put up a fight, just stood there staring into space. She tucked the gun butt under her arm and strode toward Mother and Aunt Ethel, who were still nose-to-nose. Mother's expression had slid from docile into dangerous when Aunt Ethel got in her face, and now, teeth-baring was not out of the question.

No one had even noticed Mimzie and me standing on the porch. I looked down at Mimzie again, to make sure she wasn't about to barf or faint or do something hysterical like some women do when they can't handle life. She seemed to be all right, although natural color was having difficulty coming back to her cheeks.

Out on the lawn, my three female relatives still stood clumped in an angry huddle in the middle of the yard. I looked over at Daddy. His head now hung between his outstretched arms. He stared at the floorboards, watching the ball of his foot snub out his just lit cigar. I wondered what Aunt Ethel meant by "lied to those girls every day of their lives," but I didn't really have time to think about it then. Mother was pointing her finger at Aunt Ethel and yelling, while Auntie Jeanne struggled to keep hold of the shotgun and pry Mother and Aunt Ethel apart at the same time.

"This is none of your business," Mother screamed with that high-pitched edge to her voice that made you wince involuntarily. "They are our children and how we choose to raise them is none of your concern."

"It's abuse, plain and simple," Aunt Ethel hollered back. "I should call the authorities. Those girls have the right to know who they are. You think they won't figure it out? You think they are stupid, with the two of you arguing over them all the time? And now with Jeanne moving back down here with Mimzie. You've got to tell them. You have got to come clean."

"Now, Ethel," Auntie Jeanne started, rearing back like she was considering the advantages of bringing the nose of the shotgun up to Ethel's eye level. "I'm starting to agree with Melba here. You're over-stepping your bounds. You are headed to the point of no return."

I had been so transfixed on what my mother and aunts were saying that I hadn't even checked on poor Uncle Jed. The motion of Daddy coming to his feet caught my attention. My eyes followed his and we watched Uncle Jed shimmy up the trunk of the oak tree. He lifted his foot high, placing it in the indentions where the oak's great arms reached toward the house. Grasping the wide limbs, Jed eased himself higher into the branches. If it had been summer with thick foliage intact, we wouldn't have been able to see him, but his red flannel shirt stood in marked contrast against the almost naked branches of the tree.

"Jed?" Daddy said. He didn't shout this, but he said it loud enough to silence Mother and my aunts. All eyes now followed Daddy's.

A wail escaped Aunt Ethel. "Jed, Jed baby. What are you doing? Come down, honey. Please come back down." She rushed to the base of the tree and hugged it, looking up. Mother and Auntie Jeanne stared, motionless.

"Leave me alone, all of y'all," Jed yelled down. "Go on inside and stop your bickering, or I'll jump. I can't take this anymore. I'll jump. I swear I'll jump."

Mother heated up leftovers for supper. Keeping busy had always been her way to avoid confrontation, to avoid life. Auntie Jeanne had taken Mimzie upstairs for a little pow-wow after we came back inside. I wished Mother would take me upstairs for one. Questions buzzed around in my head like a swarm of hungry bees. What did Aunt Ethel mean? No one was abusing me. How could me living a happy life with my family add up to anything close to abuse? And why would I need the right to know who I was? I knew. Didn't I? And what lies? I wanted to know . . . what lies.

I remembered Mimzie's boldness at dinner. I wished for some of it now. I wanted to walk right up to my mother and ask her what Aunt Ethel meant, but like Uncle Jed, I was paralyzed, glued to the floor by the fear of knowing the truth. Mother always said, "The truth is only good when it doesn't hurt." Her silence now spoke volumes. I couldn't convince my feet to take the steps.

I stared into the back yard through the dining room window. Darkness now draped the old oak tree, but the porch light caught in the lens of Uncle Jed's glasses, illuminating his pale face like a ghostly presence watching in the night. How could he stay up there so long? It might get chilly. He needed to come in. What was so horrible about down here that made him prefer sitting in a tree to being with us?

I turned when I heard the front door open. Daddy had gone out for awhile after we all came back in the house from the yard. He glanced my way and smiled, but it wasn't his usual smile, full of mischief and life. Now it was sad, a sad smile, like he'd lost something precious, but was trying to buck up and accept it with grace.

"Come to supper," Mother announced, sticking her head out of the kitchen just long enough to get the words out, then ducking back into her oven-heated retreat. I wandered to the kitchen table and pulled out a chair. Daddy came in and took up his usual place, newspaper in hand. His hiding place had always been behind the morning edition's editorial section, even if it was late in the day. Mother busied herself, moving casserole dishes from the oven, and filling bowls with gumbo again. Somehow, my favorite holiday recipe had now lost its appeal. I hadn't seen Aunt Ethel since we came back inside, but I glanced out the kitchen window and noticed her heavyset figure rocking on the back porch. I guessed she felt like she couldn't come inside either, since Uncle Jed refused to come down.

When Auntie Jeanne and Mimzie entered the room, a hot silence hung so thick and charged around us I wondered if Mother had added a big dash of Cayenne pepper to the air. Auntie Jeanne kept her head low, not making eye contact with anyone, but Mimzie held hers high, her chin jutting out as if daring someone, anyone to knock her out with an uppercut to the jaw. Our eyes met. Hers looked red, like they had cried. She nodded toward me with a stiff smile. I wanted to blurt out, "What is it? You got something to tell me, just spill it. I can't take this silence anymore." But I just nodded back. I knew Auntie Jeanne had explained things to her, and it hurt. What made Mimzie so special? Why couldn't someone do the same for me?

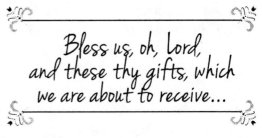

*Bless us, oh, Lord, and these thy gifts, which we are about to receive...*

Chairs scraped across the linoleum. Everyone settled into the seats. Daddy lifted his fingers to his forehead. "In the name of the Father and of the Son and of the Holy Spirit, Amen." We chanted our usual mealtime prayer, but at the end of it, Daddy cleared his throat and brushed the hair off his forehead. "And Lord, give us the strength and the love for one another to survive this most recent of unpleasant ordeals. Amen."

Everyone crossed themselves and mumbled, "Amen," but when the dishes were cleared, the plates and bowls were still full of food.

I could hardly wait to go to bed, partly because I wanted to talk to Mimzie alone and partly because I felt numb from the day. Uncle Jed still hadn't come down from the tree, and Aunt Ethel only came in long enough to grab an afghan and a cup of coffee. She and Mother glared at each other the whole time she was in the house, but didn't say a word. Last I checked, Aunt Ethel was snuggled up on the porch swing, camping out until her husband either came down, fell out or jumped out of his tree.

I stepped into my baby doll pajamas and crawled into bed. I undid my pigtails while I waited for pokey Mimzie to finish in the bathroom and join me. I had waited about as long as I could stand. By the time my bedroom door closed behind her, I had so many pent up questions I blurted them all out at once.

"Okay, so talk. What did your mother tell you? Did she explain what Aunt Ethel meant? What's all this talk about lies? Who is lying? And what are they lying about? I have to know. I want to know, Mimzie, so talk."

She pulled her hairbrush from her overnight case and dragged it slowly through her chocolate hair. She settled onto her bed, her long Barbie nightgown pulled up so she could sit Indian style. "Your mother doesn't tell you much, does she?" she asked, pausing for a minute, her hairbrush resting in her lap.

"Tell me about what?"

"Life, your life, our lives."

I didn't like where she was headed. I bit back, "I don't know what you mean. What's there to tell?"

She started brushing again, slow strokes that started at the top of her head and slid ever so slowly down past her shoulders and the length of her hair. Her knowing expression gave me a shiver. For the first time I realized that she knew about the lies, she had known all along. None of Aunt Ethel's words had confused her. This smug little so-and-so who had come into my house as a visitor, a stranger, knew more about my family and me than I knew myself.

"We're sisters," she said, as if it were common knowledge. Without the slightest hint of distress in her voice, she acted like this edict's impact would be minimal, if it held a blow at all. I stared straight into her eyes. She didn't blink. I found no malice there, but there was something. I couldn't decipher if it was coming from friend or foe.

"Sisters?" I asked, unable to come up with anything better. Air burned as it entered my lungs. I looked down and played with the satin edge of my bed blanket like I'm sure I did as a small child. I blinked back betraying tears and my brain buzzed in my ears.

Mimzie's weight depressed the edge of my bed. She rested her hand on my arm. "I thought you knew," she said, "when I got here this morning. I thought you were giving me such a hard time because I was moving in on your territory. I thought you hated me because I was coming to live here, that you didn't want me as your sister. That's why I was such a snit."

I couldn't look up. I knew I would start screaming, "Liar, liar, pants on fire," or worse, crying like a baby who had been dropped on her head. I couldn't understand what I was hearing. I refused to believe that my own mother hadn't told me, refused to tell me that I had a sister, or that this sister was coming to live with us, coming to stay.

"You're staying?" is all I managed.

She nodded, looking away.

My blood pulsed and throbbed across my forehead like a river of pain. "Let me get this straight. My mother is your mother, too? No, this is crap. What about Auntie Jeanne? She's not . . ."

"No, I've known for a long time that she's not my 'real mother,' she calls it. But I don't know about the rest."

I couldn't just sit there. I had to move, but I couldn't get up. Mimzie's weight on the covers held me captive in my own bed. I yanked the pillows out from behind

me, propped them up and leaned back into them, my arms crossed across my chest. I must say, at this point, I was a bit relieved. At least my life was still intact. If, for whatever reason, my mother had given Mimzie up to Auntie Jeanne to raise, well, that action didn't have a direct impact on me. At least she'd kept me. My mother was still mine. I would just have to get used to sharing her with Mimzie, the lesser of all the evils I had imagined thus far. But suddenly, the other half of the equation splattered across my mind like the gush of a severed vein. "What about Daddy?"

"That I haven't figured out yet," she said.

I snapped my head up, looking daggers at her. "What? You don't know? But I thought . . ."

"No, Mommy . . . or uh, I guess I should call her Auntie Jeanne now that we're here . . ." Mimzie started, but stopped. Tears welled up in her eyes. She pinched them closed and I watched as her defiant nature struggled to regain control. It took only seconds, and finally she managed to squelch any possibility of emotion. Facial features that had started out softer than I had seen them yet tightened into the familiar mask of a miniature prizefighter that had learned the hard way to grin and bear it and to turn the other cheek. I tried not to, but I felt bad for this girl. I didn't want to share my pity party, but she was obviously hurting, too. Maybe Mother was right—the truth isn't all it is cracked up to be.

"Let's just say," she continued, "I know more than you do, but that's not enough. I want all the answers and I will get them, Aza Claire. If I have to burn this damn house down to do it, I'll get the answers I need." She stood up, clinching and re-clinching her fists, walked to the door and flipped off the overhead light. Her slippers slapped across the floor, then I heard sheets rustle as she climbed into bed. "One thing we know for sure," she whispered in the darkness.

"What's that?" I muttered, my mind still filing through this new information like I had been handed papers marked, *Top Secret, Do Not Divulge.*

"We are sisters. They wouldn't have told me that much if it weren't true."

"I suppose," I replied to the dark, bruised that *they* had told her and not me.

"I don't know about you, but that means a lot to me. That means that we are blood. And nothing comes between blood."

I swallowed hard, but couldn't even get out the words, "I suppose."

As a young girl I used to struggle to stay awake on Christmas Eve so I could get a glimpse of Santa, but I never succeeded. I always nodded off, and then awoke in the morning, wondering why I couldn't stay awake for just that one night. This Christmas Eve, however, I prayed for sleep. All I wanted was a blanket of slumber to fall on me, to knock me out, to bury me under its heavy fog where no one could hurt me, where thoughts could not surface to take me deeper into the waves of *what if?* I no longer cared about Santa. I tossed and fought my bedclothes, my baby dolls kept riding up and getting tangled under my arms, and I wanted the night to end so I could give up the struggle, but I also feared what revelations morning would surely bring.

Over and over in my head I rehearsed the speech I planned to accost my mother with at breakfast. "Tell me, just tell me. I have a right to know who I am, if I have a sister, if you're really my mother, if Daddy is my Daddy, or if my life has been one big, long lie." Finally, sometime before the hint of dawn, I floated on the cusp of dreams, where consciousness tells you, "You're awake. This is real," and subconscious beckons, "Come with me. It's a dream." I heard the window open. It squeaked like it always did when I climbed out onto the roof of the front porch to watch the stars. I thought it must be my best friend, come for a visit, but wondered why she would come in through our escape hatch. And on Christmas Eve? *Or maybe it's Daddy,* I thought, *dressed up like Santa to surprise me.* He used to dress up every year, but had stopped when moths dined on his costume and left it tattered and holey; Mother wouldn't let him wear it after that.

*"Hush little babies, don't say a word . . ."*

*Ah, how sweet,* I thought, *still dreamy. Daddy is serenading me.* He didn't want me to be scared. He's come to sing me a lullaby like he did when I was a little kid.

*"Papa's gonna buy you a mockingbird . . ."*

No, Daddy, I thought. Didn't you read my list? I don't want a bird. I want a new Go-Go Barbie Convertible, and a Skipper with red hair and a white dog. A new transistor radio might be nice, too. I struggled to pry my sleep-dazed eyes open.

*"If that mockingbird don't sing . . ."*

Ouch! Why would Daddy punch me in the arm?

"Aza Claire, wake up," he said in a voice not quite his own. My eyelids fluttered, then opened, but it was Mimzie's face staring down into mine, her eyeballs wide and out on a stem. "Wake up, you ninny. Look. Look."

*"Papa's gonna buy you a diamond ring . . ."*

I pushed up onto my elbows, my mind still reeling between reality and my dreams. The room was dark. Crickets chirped so loudly it was as if they had moved in with us. I followed Mimzie's gesture toward the window. My chiffon curtains billowed around a skinny Santa, not Daddy at all, who was sitting on the floor, just inside. I rubbed sleep away and hair out of my face, and looked again. This strange Santa reshaped itself into the body of Uncle Jed. He sat on the hardwoods, hugging his knees with red flannel arms, and rocked back and forth to his *Hush Little Baby* tune.

*"If that diamond ring turns brass . . ."*

"Uncle Jed?" My pasty tongue stuck to the roof of my mouth. I worked up some spit and said it again. "Uncle Jed? What are you doing in here? You okay?"

*"Papa's gonna buy you a looking glass . . ."*

"What's wrong with him?" Mimzie whispered. She clung to me like a scaredy cat. "Is he crazy or something?"

*"If that looking glass gets broke . . ."*

"No, no, he's just a little slow, that's all. He wouldn't hurt a fly." I kept my voice low so as not to upset him. "It's okay, Uncle Jed. It's me, Aza Claire." I crawled over Mimzie, pulling my comforter with me as I moved toward the window. I squatted in front of my uncle and draped the downy cover over him, tucking it in around his shoulders. He looked up into my eyes and smiled.

"I promised I'd never tell," he said, holding my gaze. He grabbed my hand, the comforter's fabric a cushion between us, keeping our flesh from touching. He brought the bundle to his lips and kissed it. "Now that Ethel let the cat out, Sisters won't be mad at me no more."

"Let the cat out about what?" I asked.

"I'm so glad you're both here now. My little girls. I've wanted to sing you this song for so long."

His words slapped me. *His little girls?* No, I thought, not his! A force of realization struck me. I lost my balance and fell back onto my rump, backing away, pushing away, as the weight of the day and the horror held within his words spiraled around me. Tears pooled on my lower lids, threatening to overflow the rims.

"What did he say?" Mimzie shrieked, high and shrill like a stepped upon mouse.

But I couldn't think about her now. Only my life held importance. Only my parents mattered now. I clambered to my feet, grabbed for my bed, the door, anything to hold onto, anything to take me away. "No, no." The strangled words escaped me. "But how? How? You're not. No, you're not *my* father!" I yanked at the doorknob and flung open the door. It banged against the wall. "Mother, Mo . . . ther," I yelled and flew down the hall toward my parent's room. "Wake up, whoever you are. Wake up and talk to me, NOW!"

I fell through my parent's bedroom door, panting like I had run a race, but scanning the room, I realized they weren't in their bed. I bolted down the dark hallway, almost knocking Mimzie down as I pushed past her and headed down the stairs, all the while feeling slashed by serrated filaments of the lie I had been forced to live. My youth and sketchy understanding of human reproduction didn't take any logical leaps. Innocence insulated me from what this revelation could really mean. Instead, I felt a slippage, Daddy sliding down a muddy hill away from me, being melted into its brownness like the scary whisper of a dream you can't drag back from the edge of loss, and Uncle Jed's slack face and clumsiness moving toward me, trudging through the thickness with sure and stilted steps, his slowness taking hold of my mind, my hope, my breath, to pull me against him. I resisted, fought the image, but couldn't seem to yank myself away. Was I really this man's daughter? If so, what did that mean? Would I lose Daddy forever? Would he vanish from the house or move away? Simple childlike worries flashed before me. Who would read the morning paper? Would the house lose the bitter sweetness of Daddy's beloved cigars? Then Uncle Jed's slowness shocked my senses. Was I like him? Had I always been? Had I inherited his mental problems? Another secret? Was I retarded and didn't know?

At the bottom of the stairs I found Mother and Daddy in the living room, arranging presents under the Christmas tree. Startled by my abrupt entrance, their stricken faces seemed frozen in mid-exclamation. Mother finally murmured, "Not yet, Aza, dear. It's too early. Santa hasn't been here yet," and she went back to her present straightening chore, as if unaffected by my distress.

"Arrgh!" I threw up my hands and headed for the door. The foyer spit me out onto the front lawn and the bruised haze of predawn darkness swallowed me up. I had nowhere to go, but set out anyway. Getting away seemed my only choice. I took off down the street toward a friend's house, panting with every step, ignoring Daddy's call from the porch, until the houses blurred in my periphery and a chill of numbness caused my bare feet to ache. At the corner I stopped, abrupt and determined, and looked both ways like the good girl I no longer wanted to be. That's when a hand touched my shoulder. On reflex I spun round to attack. It was Mimzie. She ducked away from my right cross, and then caught my hand on the recoil. Tears glistened on her cheeks like sleet pellets on the face of an unsuspecting violet on a raw winter day. We just stood there, staring at each other, cast off dolls without a mother, and no father we wanted to claim. There was nothing we could say at that point. Only stare. Only pant. Only pray.

Seconds passed with no comment or motion, but finally an answer came to me. Right or wrong, it didn't matter. I had to move. I grabbed her by the shoulder of her nightgown as a feeble plan of action unfolded like a soggy map of redemption inside my head. I yanked. She followed. And we set out together down the street.

After sneaking through the backyards of several houses, we squeezed through the boxwood hedge encircling our yard and crept around behind Uncle Jed's . . . ur uh . . . *that man's* wounded truck. The great oak limb still protruded from its windshield. We ducked down to keep out of sight. Lights blared from every window of the house. The side

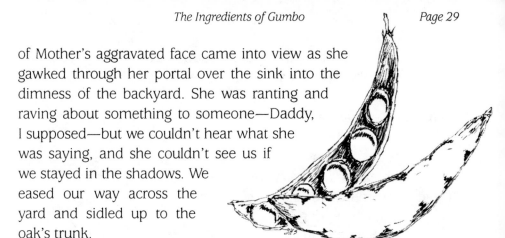

of Mother's aggravated face came into view as she gawked through her portal over the sink into the dimness of the backyard. She was ranting and raving about something to someone—Daddy, I supposed—but we couldn't hear what she was saying, and she couldn't see us if we stayed in the shadows. We eased our way across the yard and sidled up to the oak's trunk.

Mimzie said in a husky whisper, "What are we going to do now?"

I had no idea all of the sudden. Plan? What plan? I was lost. I glanced upward for heavenly assistance. Rays of moonlight burst into a prism of silver chards, daggers of light that pierced the oak's branches above our heads and reached down toward us.

"I was afraid you were going to suggest that," Mimzie said glumly, but she impressed me when she reached for the lowest branch, lifted her bare foot, and said, "I'll need a leg up."

My toes gripped the cool bark as I climbed behind her. About fifteen feet up, we nestled into two crooks where the tree's largest arms broke away from the trunk and unfurled themselves in a river of smaller branches reaching out toward the house.

"We'll wait," I said finally.

"For what?"

"The truth, the whole truth and nothing but the truth." Secretly I hoped we'd be discovered soon. My teeth had decided a drum roll might punctuate our situation nicely. A shiver began in my rib cage and rattled me so fiercely the tree seemed to vibrate against my back. Baby doll nighties weren't made for tree climbing or for winter weather, even a Louisiana winter. I wanted to be back in bed and for the night to start over from the beginning so I could sleep away the parts that had irrevocably altered my life.

A sudden chorus of adult shouts rang out from the front yard. "Mim . . . zie! Aza Cla . . . ire! Come back, girls. We need to talk." Everyone was outside now, looking for us. Their yells echoed through the cool night air. I glanced over at Mimzie, who struggled to hold on to her "willing to stick it out" face while blowing warm air into her hands.

"Not such a great idea, huh?" I admitted, looking down.

"'Desperate situations deserve desperate measures,'" she assured me. "I read that somewhere. Fits this situation just right, I think. Don't you?"

The crunching sound of leaves underfoot alarmed us. We searched the ground below us, but saw no one. Then we heard the scraping sound of bark against heavy leather behind us. We strained and wiggled to discover its source, but our precarious positions kept us from moving about too much.

"Hi, y'all!" Uncle Jed's index finger punched the back of my shoulder. He was standing on the branch directly opposite from mine on the other side of the massive trunk. "What y'all doing up here? Can I play?"

"We're not playing. This is serious business," Mimzie said, craning her neck to make eye contact with him. I stared forward. I didn't want to look at him. I just wanted to vaporize. "You aren't really our father, are you?"

"Why, sure I am," he said. "But Sisters said it'd be better if they raised you. I ain't done a day's paid work in my life, ya know. Nobody'll hire me. Can't afford no kids, they said. But I think they think I'm too slow."

"Who is our mother then?" Mimzie asked.

"Oh, well, um . . ." There was silence for a moment. I wondered if he would answer at all. Then a wail so tragic burst from him I thought a great, gnarled hand had reached inside him, grabbed his heart and yanked it out of his chest, ripping flesh and breaking bone to get it out.

"Oh, no, it's okay," Mimzie said in a panic. She scrambled toward him on her branch. She couldn't reach far enough around the trunk to touch him, so she fought to stand up, but lost her footing and almost fell. I tried to steady her and turn to see him at the same time, but couldn't maneuver well on the limb. Once Mimzie regained her balance, I slumped forward to hug my branch and hold my ears. His howl finally subsided into gusty moans. Through snuffles and hiccuppy sobs, he managed, "She died birthing you. She's an angel now. I see her sometimes, but she never saw you, never got to hold you at all."

It was clear from Mimzie's expression that she could see him clearly and he was looking her straight in the eye. The light within her darkened sharply. She blinked, taking the blame, absorbing the responsibility for our mother's death. The shame settled in on her heart. Before I could do anything to help her, footsteps drew our attention to the ground. Mother, Daddy, Auntie Jeanne and Ethel must have heard the explosion of Jed's heartache. They were now gathered below us, looking up with pleading eyes.

"Oh, heck, might as well go in," I said, dejected, and I glanced over at Mimzie, feeling like life might be easier if we just leaned sideways and fell to the cold, hard ground. "Come on, Jed. Want some cocoa? I could sure use some. What about you, Mimz?"

The glow of Christmas tree lights did nothing to brighten our moods as Mimzie and I sipped our hot cocoa in the living room on the couch. Mimzie hadn't uttered a word since we came down from the tree. Mother had draped us with a knitted afghan. Then she set about her task of pacing a raw spot through the Oriental runner behind the couch, while Daddy busied himself straightening presents under the tree again. Aunt Ethel had taken Uncle Jed upstairs to calm him down, and Auntie Jeanne was still in the kitchen fussing with the cocoa mess.

"You're a liar, nothing but a liar," I said under my breath, just loud enough for Mother to hear. I hoped my words would reach behind me and slap her up side of the head, hurt her as much as they hurt me to say them. I wheeled around and met her sad gaze. "Why didn't you tell us? How could you lie to us about all of this?"

"I . . . We . . ." Mother stammered for the first time I could recall. She moved around to face us and perched on the edge of the coffee table, her knees almost touching ours.

I didn't give her the chance to collect enough words for a sentence. "Mimzie is my sister! And I find this out when I'm ten! How could you not tell me? I have a sister, a sister, for Christ's sake."

"Now, Aza dear, please listen . . ."

"And Daddy, ooooh, Daddy. Who is he?" Daddy peeped up at me from his kneeling place by the tree and I thought I saw a tear in his eye. He looked back down before I could be sure. I didn't care when waterworks exploded from me like bottle rockets and streamed down my cheeks. Mother's face blurred and the Christmas lights muddied into long streaks of luminous liquid in my eyes. "Uncle Jed is *not* our father. Tell us none of this is true."

Mother reached her hand across the narrow void between us. I pulled away.

"No, sweetie, no, you don't understand."

Sudden and blinding rays of the overhead light startled us and filled the dim room. My arm flew up to cover my eyes. Mother and Daddy winced.

"What's going on now?" Auntie Jeanne shouted, stepping into the room. "Haven't we had enough upset for one night?" Her words sliced the air and cut off the circulation to my anger. Mimzie moved in closer beside me to shore us up with a supportive hand in mine. But it was Auntie Jeanne's turn now. "Hold on, everyone just hold on." She moved to the center of the room behind Mother, who then rose, walked to the fireplace and leaned against it hard enough to keep the walls from falling down. Silence encompassed the room for a moment. Only ragged breaths and tearful gasps held us up. "Mimzie, dear," Auntie Jeanne continued in a more even tone, "tell me calmly what else happened tonight to cause all this." She raked a hand through a mass of sleep-tangled hair.

Mimzie faltered for a second or two, then straightened her shoulders and sidled up to me under our afghan as if we'd been joined at the heart our whole lives. "We know we are sisters—you told me that much— then Uncle Jed climbed in our bedroom window and announced that he is our father. And then, in the tree . . . he, well, he said . . ." She swallowed hard. "It's not true, is it? Tell us. It's confession time. Aza Claire and I deserve the whole truth."

Auntie Jeanne looked over at Mother with resignation in her eyes.

"It is time, Melba. It's way past time. To hell with all your Southern gentility, pride and secrets. Cough it up. If you won't do it, I will."

Mother's strength gave way. She crumpled into a hysterical heap onto the hearth, crushing the brightly colored packages strewn at her feet. "I'm so, so sorry," she cried, her face buried in her hands. "We wanted to do what was right, what was best. We love you. We only wanted you both to have good lives, happy lives." Auntie Jeanne stepped over presents to get to Mother, then she squatted down and placed her hand on Mother's leg. Daddy slumped into the Queen Anne chair by the Christmas tree, his head in his hands. "Jed was doing so much better," Mother continued through her tears. "He had been living at the Home and working at the shoe factory real regular for a couple of years. When they let him move into the group home, everybody thought he would do fine. The doctors assured us that he would be all right, that he'd handle it well."

Mimzie and I leaned forward, drawn by the reality we didn't want to hear. We scooted involuntarily to the edge of the sofa, hanging onto one another as if releasing might cause us both to collapse. Our eyes were glued on the faces of these two strangers, the women we had known as our mothers until today.

"He is our brother," Auntie Jeanne interjected, her voice strained an octave above any that exist. "We'd do anything for him, even raise his children and love them as our own."

Mother lifted her head to look at me, but when our eyes met, she got so choked up she couldn't speak. She mouthed, "I love you, Aza dear."

"Jed loved your mother." Auntie Jeanne picked up the story. She told it to the floor. "She was such a sweet little thing. Had Down's syndrome, the poor dear. They wanted to live together, she and Jed, and get married. They wanted to have their little life and family, but the authorities wouldn't let them. They said our dear Jed had taken advantage of her and of the situation, but he didn't. He couldn't. The sweet man couldn't take advantage of anybody if he tried."

"But Aunt Ethel? Who is she . . .?" I asked.

"She was the house mother at the group home," Mother said, and rooted around in her robe pocket for a tissue. "They fired her for letting it happen. It was Ethel's job to keep watch over the residents. She tried, I'm sure, but Jed was so in love, so head over heels in love."

"Then how did Jed and Ethel get together?" Mimzie managed to spit coherent words out that my brain couldn't even wrap thoughts around.

But before she could answer, Mother's tear-pinched expression softened suddenly. She looked past us, her eyes focused on something behind us, above our heads. Mimzie and I turned to see Aunt Ethel and Uncle Jed standing in the entry hall, entwined in each other's arms. Uncle Jed stared at something only he could recognize or see in his mind's own outer space. His head rested on Ethel's chubby shoulder, content and calm for the moment. Ethel's soothing hands made tiny circles across his shoulders and along his back as if rubbing love into a favorite rag doll.

"I didn't do my job. I didn't take care of the sweet, dear people in my care," Ethel whispered. "I loved them all, love them still, but back then I let them down."

"I love you, too," Uncle Jed said too loudly. He lifted his head ever so slightly, then replaced it gently back onto her shoulder.

Ethel ran her fingers over the top of his head. "I know, love. I know you do. Now, hush. Everything is going to be okay." She lifted her chin and shook her hair out of her face. "It's true, girls—Jed is your father. Your real mother, bless her heart, well, I'm sorry I can't tell you more about her. It was wrong of me to get all riled up earlier. I wanted to prevent just this from happening. Now, look what a mess I've caused. These women, your mothers here, although I might not agree with them on some things, have done their best. Jed always knew you girls were his. And I knew if your mothers didn't tell you, Jed would—like he did tonight. I was afraid for you, afraid of you getting hurt, but mostly, I was afraid for him."

Silence fell upon us. What else was there to say? What else could anyone do? Mimzie and I took turns staring into the faces of our family, such as they were. After what seemed like eternity, Mimzie and I stood up together and plodded back upstairs to our room, leaving the adults to clean up the mess.

Now, many Christmases later, I sit at the same dining room table, watching my family file in and take their usual seats. Hard to believe eight years have passed. The first thing Mimzie does is kick her shoes off under the table, but thankfully, her feet remain on the floor. Aunt Ethel and Uncle Jed mosey in, arm in arm. Ethel is chattering to him about how watching too much television will harm his eyes. Once everyone is settled, Daddy says grace and Mother lifts Great-grandma Vermaelen's silver soup ladle to fill our bowls. I think about gumbo a lot these days, every time I watch Mimzie shovel big spoonfuls of it into her prissy little mouth. I guess her Southern blood won out over her Yankee upbringing. Not surprising, if you ask me. She and Auntie Jeanne did, in fact, move south to stay. And poor Daddy. Auntie Jeanne always beats him to the morning paper. He has nowhere to hide now. I guess you could say we survived our "latest of troubling upsets," as Mother calls it. And yes, in case you're wondering, I still claim her as the closest thing I've got to a maternal relative.

> *Names, names, names. I am fascinated by names. Have you ever known someone with the wrong name? Not me. Hmm, I wonder where I came up with these!*

Mimzie now claims Mother and Auntie Jeanne both.

It all seems kind of funny when I think about it. On that warm, humid Christmas Eve all those years ago, when our seemingly normal heritage took on the looks and personality of the proud centuries of screwed up Southern ancestries before us, neither one of us thought to ask the other obvious question. How did we (supposedly one year apart in age) both get born if the authorities at its discovery severed our parent's love affair? We had asked all kinds of questions about our mother, what happened to her, how she died, but our age difference didn't register in our overtaxed minds until after presents had been opened that morning and Mimzie and I had gone upstairs to get dressed for Christmas Day brunch. It dawned on us at the same instant. We thundered down the stairs once again, brimming with what we hoped would be the last unanswered question about our lives. Mother glanced up from her January issue of *Southern Belle* magazine, her eyes peeping over the rims of her dollar store reading glasses.

"Why you're twins, of course," she said bluntly, and seemed exasperated by our inability to figure it out for ourselves. "You're not a-thing alike, but you're twins just the same."

Mimzie and I studied each other's face for a few awkward seconds, stunned by the revelation of a connection so intimate, so sublime. I reached out and took her hand. Our fingers entwined. "Twins," I said. A weak smile drew up the corners of my mouth. "We're twins."

"Well, I'll be damned," she whispered.

Mother tisked and shook her finger at Mimzie, and said, "You really do need to clean up that mouth of yours, my dear."

We both threw back our heads and howled in unison, "Well, we'll be damned."

# Judy Vermaelen's Chicken & Sausage Gumbo

(Note: This is not just any gumbo recipe. This is a true Louisiana gumbo and it takes time, patience and love to make it.)

<u>First you make your chicken stock.</u>

Place chicken and next 7 ingredients in large stockpot and cover with water.

1 plump chicken, cleaned and whole

2 medium onions, chopped

6 ribs of celery, chopped

2 green bell peppers, chopped (Judy doesn't put green pepper in her gumbo
　　　because her daughter, Jeanne, doesn't like them. If you like them, go for it.)

1 whole garlic clove, minced

1½ tablespoons garlic powder

1 tablespoon salt

½ tablespoon black pepper

Boil until chicken is tender and falls off the bone, about 2 hours. Remove chicken from stock liquid, straining out the skin and bones with slotted spoon. Chop or pull chicken into pieces and set aside. Suck off any floating fat from stock liquid and strain off any nasty, slimy stuff. Leave stock in pot and keep hot until roux is ready.

(continued on next page)

# Chicken & Sausage Gumbo (continued)

<u>Next, you make the roux.</u>
1½ cups vegetable oil
1½ cups flour

In cast iron pot, combine vegetable oil and flour. Cook over low to medium heat, adjusting temperature as needed and stirring constantly with wooden spoon until mixture turns a deep, rich brown color. The second it looks brown enough, take it off the heat or it will burn!!

<u>Next the magic happens.</u>
1 pound smoked sausage
  (may use andouille sausage,
  if you prefer)
2 tablespoons filé
½ cup chopped parsley

> Judy told me that her last batch of roux took 50 minutes to reach the perfect hue. God teaches the virtue of patience in many ways. Offer this time up for the souls in Purgatory and it won't seem nearly as long.

Add roux to hot chicken stock, stirring until combined. (Do not add the stock to the roux or you'll be dealing with lumps and, believe me, you do not want lumpy gumbo.) Add smoked sausage, filé and parsley. Cook 1½ hour. Then add chicken and cook another hour or so.

While gumbo simmers, cook 8 cups of white, long grain rice in a rice cooker to assure perfect tenderness.

To serve, sprinkle cooked rice with filé in a bowl and spoon gumbo over rice. Do not put filé on top of the gumbo; it just doesn't taste right in that order.

Enjoy and be proud of yourself for loving your family enough to spend the time it takes to make great gumbo!

# A Pause in Mid-Sentence

Writing flashes vaporize
from my fingertips, moving too
quickly to be caught by the hand.
My office door opens,
the feeble gate between maternal
bliss and my heaven of lexis.
In blatant disobedience, her whisper
cracks my air of meditation,
shattering it around me in
sentence fragments,
dangling participles that fall
to my keyboard like filament in
search of the lost thought,
the vanquished word.

I know you're working, but . . .
The anomaly of <u>but</u> strikes
me like a feather across the face.
Can we build a tent?
I want to paint.
Let's jump on the trampoline.
Teach me needlepoint.
Where are my shoes?

Two a.m. fate settles on my
hunched shoulders like
a granny shawl. I smile at
the blessed displeasure,
save to file and close, knowing
words only travel by Interstate in
the early hours of inspiration, when
their headlights blind me with
paragraphs of whole thought,
and when wee ones are snuggly
tucked in their beds, dreaming of
future interruption,
and when my office door
has no need of a latch.

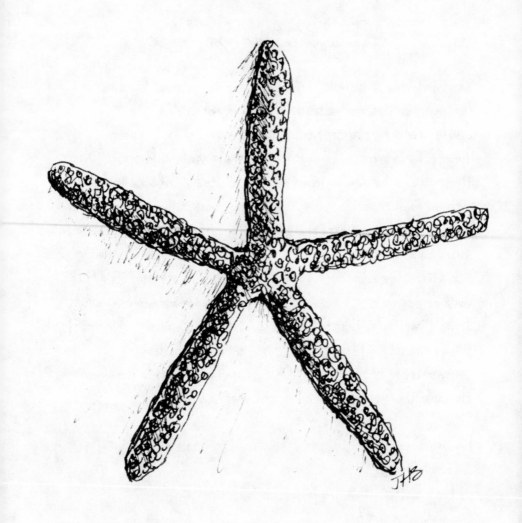

# Oma Moves In

*(Published in the National Gallery of Writing 2010,
by the West Tennessee Writing Project at University of Tennessee, Martin)*

I became someone else the day my grandmother moved in. "Call her Oma," my mother said as we drove toward the airport. "You call her Oma, and I'll call her Mom . . . I guess." Lack of airplane ticket funds, or the sharp increase in gas prices, or the decrease in speed limits due to the gas embargo had kept my grandmother in De Leon Springs exile for the first ten years of my life. One of those reasons, or something else. Then, in a startling shift, the debilities of diabetes chose now to unite us. "We'll deal with it," Mother said, readjusting herself in the car seat. "I'll deal with it. Somehow."

Announcements boomed over the airport intercom. My father jingled his keys. Mother chewed the inside of her lip. I worried the ragged fringe of my cut-offs. From the look on my father's face as we watched this stranger struggle up the Delta gangway, and before that in the car with his pronouncements—"the old Battle Ax," "Attila, the Housefrau," "that's what they make nursing homes for"—I was sure this new "warden" would make my life even more miserable than it had been so far.

My mother had never divulged the source of her pain. She never told me that her mother had had her "late in life," like she'd had me. Or about Oma leaving, about being abandoned, about waking one morning as a ten-year-old girl to discover her mother's luggage packed, left by the front door—her mother already gone. She never told me that her mother had stayed away for seven months, vanished into the heat vapors of summer. Or how her mother returned one rainy winter afternoon with new luggage and no coat. She also never told me about how life picked up after that, a quick breath after hiccups, as if the woman had only run out to the grocery or gone to a Christian women's luncheon and been delayed by a train. Mother had never explained.

Now watching this stranger exit the plane, premonitions clouded my mind. The airline had forced Oma to exit in a wheelchair, but much to the flight attendant's dismay, they couldn't make her place her feet on its footrests. The woman slapped over her shoulder at the hands that tried to push her.

"Stop that. I've made it through this life under my own power for eighty-three years. Don't need no sissy boy stewardess to help me get along." Her voice vibrated off the metal gangway walls and echoed toward us as if boomed through hi-fi speakers. A purse the size of an August watermelon sat in her lap, its innards gaping, medicine bottles and lacy handkerchiefs spilling out. A crocheted shawl encircled her.

Baby butt pink in Granny squares. *How appropriate*, I thought. Arthritic hands fought to grasp the chair's rubber-treaded wheels as her black leather orthopedic shoes, stretched wide by bruised ankles and bulbous feet, shuffled along, dragging her metal carriage by excruciating inches up the steep gangway incline. The flight attendant followed along, helpless to do anything but shake his head.

"Alfred, go help her," my mother urged, a look of desperation pinching the soft folds around her eyes. She had seemed pinched herself lately, since the long distance phone call from Oma's doctor saying that my grandmother could no longer live on her own. Mother's attitude had taken on a decidedly more whiny tone, almost childlike—a manner I recognized, since technically I was still one, even though I thought my maturity level ranked far above other children's my age—as if the news of her mother moving in with us had dragged her back in time to an age she was not thrilled about revisiting. She grabbed Daddy's arm and squeezed, her nails digging in.

"Oh, for Pete's sake," Daddy said with a huff. He threw his windbreaker into the nearest blue seat and followed the long row of attached vinyl that pointed the way toward Oma. He approached her from the side in a wide arc out of her reach. His face cracked into the painful semblance of a smile as he rounded her, then he patted her arm and moved behind her as the flight attendant scurried away with the speed of a mouse freed from the jaws of death. Daddy grabbed hold of the chair, ready to push. Not a smart move. Oma turned, grimaced, and slapped his hands away. Daddy shoved them into his pants pockets and followed. I'd never seen him follow anyone before.

Only moments later, I was shocked to learn that my grandmother could walk. Not the strong and strident walk of well-circulated limbs by any means, but the stifled shuffle of legs grown rigid from too little blood flow and too many years of practicing the task. I watched in amazement as she hoisted her bulky frame from the wheelchair just seconds after its treads crossed the gangway finish line. She rose to every inch of her 4-foot 11-inch frame and let out a belch so loud and gaseous people waiting to board the next flight covered their noses and struggled to suppress gasps. "That's better," she announced to anyone within earshot. "Damned airplane food. A wonder I survived a-tall. Now, get me the hell out of here." She grabbed my father's arm, much like Mother had done, so tightly he actually winced. "Walk," she commanded. I didn't recognize my father as my own when he tucked his head and obeyed.

After a long drive sandwiched in the middle of the backseat between my mother—Oma had taken over her place in the front seat—and the remaining stack of mismatched luggage that wouldn't fit into the trunk, Oma moved into my 8-by-10 foot room and became my cellmate. As my mother had warned, my best friend, Carolyn Anderson-Smith, wouldn't be spending the night again anytime soon. Oma now owned the less lumpy sibling of my twin beds. Sitting cross-legged in the middle of mine, I watched her strip off the brand new sheets and J.C. Penney comforter set Mother had painstakingly chosen and paid "way too much for" only days ago. She had used part of her grocery money for the purchase. I resented the fact that her decision had forced Chef Boy-R-Dee entrees upon us for dinner every night since. Oma tossed the never-used bed coverings aside, into a heap on the floor. She then wrenched open the first of her twenty pieces of luggage and reverently unfurled the ugliest bedspread I'd ever seen.

"My mother—your Great-grandma Eugenia—hand-crocheted this in 1888," she said, fingering the delicate threads. "She was fourteen years old at the time. I was almost two."

I had to consider this information for a moment. At ten years old, I could not imagine *ever* giving birth, but to have a child at the age of twelve "blew my mind," as Mother's hippie friends always said. At the time, I hadn't yet started my menstrual cycle, but had just completed a course in Human Health and Hygiene and realized that my great-grandmother must have given birth only moments after starting hers. I decided at that moment to become a feminist, like the "brave and rebellious women" my fifth grade teacher, Mrs. Samson, had taught us about. I was suddenly thrilled with the advances women had made over the last century or so, and vowed silently to impress Mrs. Samson with my newly discovered mission in life by writing a report on the topic for school the next week.

"Just look at this fine handwork." Oma offered the corner of the holey material for me to touch. I tucked my hands under my thighs and nodded instead. "This edging here is called tatting," she informed me, the blues of her droopy eyes delivering an electric shock when I made the mistake of meeting them directly. "A lost art, it is. Nobody does fine handwork like this anymore." She looked me up and down. "If you're smart, I'll teach you someday."

I pulled a *Tiger Beat* magazine from under my pillow and thumbed through it to a picture of David Cassidy. Then, twisting my waist-length pigtail around my finger, I leaned back into my bed pillows and pretended she wasn't there.

Oma smoothed every crease and wrinkle out of sheets so threadbare I wondered how her toenails didn't rip holes in them when she slept. Then she tugged and patted the tatted bedspread into place. I watched her backside as she did this and wondered what her undergarments must look like. Barely visible through the thin cotton print of her shirtwaist dress long ribbons of stiffness ran the length of her back. These course strips didn't bend when she bent, didn't flex at all, but I could tell her bulky body wished they would. The lace hem of a slip peeked out from beneath her skirt when she leaned forward, revealing dimpled knee backs, bruised and veiny, and opaque flesh-colored hose that were rolled into tight cords at the top of her thick calves. Her breathing labored along with her as she worked, but the soft hum of a Gospel hymn disguised the raggedness of the inhales that added a percussion beat to the mellowness of her song.

> Tatting and fine handmade crochet evolved from ancient fishnet makers' knotting techniques.
> Nuns in Cork, England were among the first to refine the art form into delicate knot-work for household use.

"Phew, ain't life wondrous," she said when she had finished, and she stretched her hands above her head to knock the kinks out. She turned to face me and flopped down on the bed, her weight disturbing its covers so violently I wondered why she had bothered to work so hard to smooth them out in the first place. I kept my eyes on my magazine, still pretending she wasn't there, but I could feel her eyes on me, hot, determined as all get-out.

"Don't talk much, do ya'?" she asked after a few minutes. And in those few she studied me more closely than my own mother had ever done.

I shrugged.

"You ain't dense or retarded, are ya'? Law, I hope not. Three of my brothers were dumb as pine stumps. The other 'leven of us was all more or less normal, though, thank the Good Lord. It'd be awful hard living in the same room with a child who can't put two words together to make a thought."

I stifled the urge to shout, "Fourteen brothers and sisters? You've got to be kidding!" Instead, I stood up abruptly in the middle of my bed. I towered above her for a minute—a dramatic pause, I like to think of it—not saying a word. Then I jumped off the end of the bed and strutted out of the room, my bell-bottomed backside swishing as I tried, but failed to impress her with how in control of my world I could be.

Later that evening my grandmother stripped down to her skivvies right in front of me. I had just returned from the hall bathroom where I had scrubbed my face with Noxzema to prevent the adolescent plague of acne that was sure to arrive any day now, and had changed into my satin Barbie gown. I stopped dead in the doorframe at the sight of her, my eyeballs out on stems. No need to wonder any longer what her undergarments looked like. She had dropped her shirtwaist dress off her shoulders and let it fall to the floor. Now, she stood in the puddle of it and was struggling to lift her full slip over her head. The lace had gotten caught on a bobby pin, one of the hundreds that secured her bluish bun at the nape of her neck. Her arms were extended heavenward as her bulky torso, girded into a stiff white jellyroll by unyielding fabric, wriggled this way and that. A train track of hooks and eyes ran from a flat expanse of elastic at her crotch upward to the cavern between her jiggling breasts. She must have sensed my presence. "Could you give me a hand?" she asked, her gyrations ceasing for the moment, her arms still extended and trapped by the beige nylon.

I was frozen, though, unable to respond, my eyes riveted on her bare thighs where empty white garter clasps dangled above blackened

flesh. Translucent skin, as crinkled and thin as Christmas present tissue paper, hung loose and sagging over her landscape of pain. Rivers and large pools of deep violet-black traversed each thigh, fading only slightly into splotchy baby puke green expanses that stretched like wide tributaries across a frail mountain of bone. The deeper bruised hues then dissolved into mustard yellow plains near her knees and around the back of her legs. Her thin cloud-cover of skin failed to disguise the tortured flesh that lay beneath it. The anguish this mottled vision emitted set my gag reflex to pulse. My hand covered my mouth. *Who could have done this to her,* I wondered. *Who could beat an old lady so mercilessly and leave her unhealed?* No answer came to me, and before my mind could deliver reason, she stirred again and flopped onto the edge of the bed from the exhaustion of holding her arms up for so long. Her words shook me. "A little help, please?"

I stammered, but didn't move forward to assist. Instead, I yelled "Mother" over my shoulder without budging, still staring. I heard my mother get up from the kitchen table. The chair scraping across linoleum put my teeth on edge. "She's coming," I said to Oma, and then with great effort, I high-stepped onto my bed and backed into the corner of my room. Standing there, my toes buried in feather down, I struggled to rip my eyes away from her legs.

When Mother entered the room, she rushed to her mother's aid, but the glare she sent my way was not lost to me. It held the bite of retribution, aimed at me as a warning of what was to come. It was scowled so viciously across my mother's face that I knew I would soon pay a high price for my lack of action. Sinking onto my bed, I yanked the covers out from under me, rolled toward the wall and covered my head.

Old people snore. I had figured this out long ago, but that first night with Oma, I gained personal knowledge of the unnerving effects rumbling, congested breathing can cause. Many night noises don't awaken a sleeper or prevent a person from the opportunity of sleep: train whistles, cricket chirps, clock ticks and Grandfather chimes. These noises often deliver a lulling quality that assists along one's trek to slumber land. But elderly snoring is a din that rivals all. Created by ornery folk, I supposed, for the sole purpose of relieving innocent bystanders of sleep.

Oma's snoring cracked my determination like a jackhammer to brain cement. It stirred up all kinds of unwelcome thoughts that made me realize just how long it had been since I last confessed my sins. I fluffed my pillow until its feathers wished they had their bird back. I flopped from side to side, unable to get comfortable and determined not to let this aggravation rule my mind or ruin my night.

All to no avail.

Around 3 a.m., I gave up and sat up in bed, my pillow now a breast shield clutched tight by my wilted arms. I turned to stare daggers at the source of my displeasure and, in the pink light of other people's dreams I witnessed something no child should ever see—death. Not real, breathless and forever gone fatality, but a demise imagined with such accuracy that the look of it was as realistic as if the family had gathered at Memorial Park Cemetery and Oma's casket cover had been raised. The glow from Mrs. Stovall's bug light across the street cast long shadows through the open weave of my pink curtains and the ghastly glow fell upon my grandmother like a misty funeral shroud. Every fold and crease in her face, of which there were many, appeared in the dimness as black slashes, gripping and grotesque. The raised flesh of her face, highlighted to the luminous crimson reserved for horror flicks, seemingly oozed with each of her ragged breaths. She didn't move under her tatted cover, but rested instead as supine as a monk upon a bed of nails in cloistered prayer.

Something odd took a hold of me in that moment. The twilight enveloped me with the cloak of understanding that is usually only granted to creatures far wiser than I. As much as I detested this woman's invasion of my life, as much as I resented her theft of my mother's attentions and patience, as much as I marveled over and feared the subordinate effect she had waged upon my father, I realized what I must do. I must put up with her. I must accept her place in my life because she would not be long in this world.

That said, however, I would keep this new wisdom to myself. It wasn't a conscious decision, more of a judgment call. I was too young to understand this innate conclusion, to grasp the self-protective reasoning behind its crystallization in my psyche. I just knew that I would not change my behavior toward her. She had not meant anything to me before her arrival; there was no need to allow her presence to impose any impression upon me now. Less to deal with after she's gone, I must have figured. I'd keep it simple. Stay separate. Out of reach.

Only five minutes of slumber had passed when my mother's hands shook me awake. It could not have been more. Her persistence dragged me back from the cloak of darkness I had prayed for and finally attained, and the fire in her eyes made it clear that payback time had arrived. A finger over her lips warned the importance of my silence. We crept out of my room, only to cross the narrow hallway into hers. The faint scent of dry roasted coffee struggled to reach us, but let me know that Daddy was in the kitchen, out of earshot.

Mother held the doorknob so it wouldn't *click* when the latch caught.

Then she moved around me as if sizing me up for the fitting of a new dress, the wheels in her head almost visible as she readied herself to commence her tirade. When she stopped the slow circular trek around me, leaning in not two inches from my nose, I did not look away. Her eyes bulged and her breath smelled of Listerine and Folgers with heavy cream. Her whispered yells delivered tiny droplets of projectile spit that misted across my face with each frenzied syllable containing a "p" or an "f." I didn't blink. I stood erect. I didn't argue or whine. I just stood there, taking what was my due like a revolutionary who'd refused a blindfold before a firing squad.

Her attack came in quick bursts. It was fueled by an anger so palpable it blotched her skin and gorged the veins in her forehead. But, when she had just hit her stride, somewhere between, "No daughter of mine is going to treat her own grandmother like trailer trash," and, "If you know what is good for you, young lady," she stopped. I sensed the presence of someone else. I didn't turn around at first, not until Mother's wide-mouthed expression in choked mid-sentence told me all I needed to know.

Oma stood in the doorway. Backlit by morning light from my bedroom window, her feeble silhouette glowed like the phantom Goddess of Grandmothers through the thin weave of her cotton nightgown. She pointed at my mother with an arthritic finger so twisted it took a left and missed its target, pointing instead toward the bureau against the far wall. She didn't say anything for a moment, just pointed, her eyes focused on my mother as if I weren't even there. Finally, with more

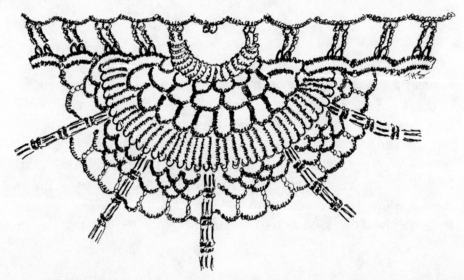

power and assurance than any word I had ever heard uttered, she said, "Don't!" That's it, just "don't." Then her crooked finger dropped to her side. She turned on a slippered heel and walked away.

When I turned back to face my mother, all color had left her face. Her chin fell to her chest. Then her fingers reached out to my shoulder as if she were going to pick a thread off a sweater or straighten a sleeve. Her fingertips tarried there, wanting to do more, then trailed down the length of my arm and grasped my hand for an instant, so briefly that my skin hardly registered the touch. "Get dressed," she said, barely audible above a whisper. She let go. "Breakfast will be ready soon."

I held the doorknob when I left so it wouldn't *click* when the latch caught hold.

They didn't hear me when I came in from school that afternoon. I headed for the kitchen to fix myself a snack, but stopped short just outside the doorway when I heard them talking. I had never eavesdropped before—our house was so tiny there had never been much need—but hearing them, I flattened myself against the wall and peered around the doorjamb with one eye. Mother was leaning over Oma, her back and side facing me. She held something in her hand. Oma was seated at the kitchen table with the hem of her skirt in a wad and clasped close to her chest.

The syringe was posed like a dagger.

"You've got to do this for me, Betty," Oma said in someone else's voice. The timbre of it had taken on a squirrel-like quality, pleading and desperate. No hint of the fierce warlord of yesterday remained. "I didn't raise you to be a queasy 'ol chicken," she was saying. "We've been at this all day, but you've got to do it this time. I've tried, but with God as my witness, I can't do it to myself."

"But Momma, I can't. I might hurt you. Oh, Lord, I think I'm going to be sick."

"Betty, just stick it in and push."

My mother wavered, shifting back and forth on feet that longed to escape. Then she leaned forward. She swabbed Oma's thigh with a moist cotton ball and a shaking hand, the syringe poised above Oma's skin like a dagger in a trembling white-knuckled fist. She searched the leg for a place to insert the needle that had not already been blackened by this daily attack, but found none.

"Just do it, Betty. Go on," Oma urged, her palm now covering her eyes.

Mother pinched up a small hunk of bruised flesh, hesitated again, then drove the needle in to its hilt, her eyelids closed so tightly only slits remained visible between her cheeks and her brows.

Oma flinched.

Mother jumped.

The needle slipped out, its contents still intact.

"Did you do it?" Oma asked, the grimace of pain still distorting her face. She peeped through her fingers and saw that the insulin was still in the syringe. "Oh, good grief!"

"I'm sorry, Momma," Mother whined. "I can't do it; I just can't." Mother rushed to the sink. It caught her gag. Oma slumped onto the table and wept.

I hated my mother after that. She was not the woman I had believed her to be. Oma's torture continued, twice daily, every morning at 9 a.m. and every evening at 7, lasting over an hour sometimes because Mother was such a wimp. Weekends were the worst; I had nowhere to escape. At least on school mornings I didn't have to listen to them: Mother whining, Oma pleading, Mother failing often and having to try again, Oma taking the abuse like a soldier captured by the Viet Cong, unwilling to give up the pleasure of her agony. (I recognized that we were a lot alike in that respect.) And then, finally, as if to punctuate Oma's misery, Mother always puked into the sink.

After a week of detached witness, I couldn't take it any longer. I had to do something, anything. I decided to rebel. I paraded into the kitchen and announced, "Carolyn is spending the night tonight. I've already asked her and her mother said it's okay." I threw open the refrigerator door, grabbed a Coke—even though I was allowed only one a day and only after I got home from school—and flopped down at a table laden with cheese grits, angel biscuits, crispy bacon, sausage patties and gravy, and homemade preserves. Two eggs over easy sputtered in a cast iron skillet on the stove.

Mother swung around, her soapy rubber-gloved hands fisting her hips. "No, Nikki, we've discussed this. No one can spend the night while Oma is staying with us. We don't have a square inch of space left in this house and no extra bed."

"That's not fair," I griped, slamming the Coke can down on the Formica with such force the carbonated liquid spewed all over my hand. "She's my best friend. You can't ruin my life like this. I hate you. I hate Oma. This isn't fair."

My words struck my mother like a snakebite to the cheek. They had never held venom before. It took her a moment to recoup, but when she did, she shot back, "You'd better watch yourself, young lady. How dare you speak to me that way?" She snatched the gloves off her hands and threw them into the sink. "I am your mother, and you will not take that tone with me." She leaned over the table. Its metal legs creaked under her weight. Shoving a chewed fingernail in my face, she said, "We've discussed this and I said, 'No sleepovers while Oma is here.' I meant it then and I mean it now. We will not have this discussion again."

I don't know what came over me. I had never dared to defy my mother, had never even thought about it. I was a good girl, usually respectful and obedient. All kids were back then, weren't we? Before Oma moved in, my mother and I had had a strained, but not particularly abnormal relationship. I tried to talk to her, sometimes, and she tried to listen. But it was as if some hereditary mutation hidden deep within our gene pool had awakened in me the moment my grandmother set foot in our house. It owned a rebellious nature and a disgruntled attitude that rubbed disorder against anything my mother or grandmother did or said. To top it all off, this attitude and its actions had taken me over. It was out of my control. Overnight my mission and duty had become defiance. I would not be pushed around. I relished the new job description.

I stood up. My chair shot backward and clattered to the linoleum as it toppled. I grasped the table's lip and lifted it off the floor, daring. I realized that another inch or so was all it would take. Another inch and bacon, sausage, grits and gravy would slide down and crash to the floor in an oozy mess at Mother's feet. Just an inch.

Mother's face melted quickly from shocked parent into fierce Banshee. But before I worked up the courage to heave, before she worked up the courage to explode, a sing-songy voice from the hallway stopped us both in mid-scream. Oma rounded the corner and paused, leaning against the doorjamb, the smile of a woman who had no intention of stooping to our level on her face. Ignoring the destruction before her, she delivered her words as if she were the only one privy to the information she shared.

"Betty, dear," she began, "Nicole has a friend coming to sleep over tonight. I'll need those beautiful linens that were on my bed when I arrived so I can fix myself up a cozy spot on the sofa. Could you get them out for me, please?" Then she strutted over to the stove, unaffected by our astonishment, and poured herself a cup of coffee. Cradling it in two hands, she turned to stare at us over its rim, her eyes dancing with mischief, her smile never wavering.

*Tick. Tick.* The tail of the kitty wall clock kept time with our silence like a stranded metronome. No one moved. No one dared to speak. It was as if all the air had evaporated from the room. *Whoosh.* In an elderly millisecond, oxygen evacuated the premises, leaving us gasping and wondering if we'd ever breathe again.

Finally, Mother collapsed back onto the cabinets for support, as if holding herself upright took too much effort. She still hadn't uttered a word. And me, well, my mind struggled but failed to make sense of it all. What *had* just happened? How *had* my grandmother pulled this off? I couldn't come up with a single constructive or destructive thing to say, so after what seemed like three days of suppression in Purgatory, I mustered up the nerve to turn and leave the room.

In my bedroom, I stared out the window. Hard as I tried, I couldn't figure it out. Why would she do that for me? What had I ever done for her? Twice this woman had interceded on my behalf. No one had ever done that for me before. But I couldn't let this little twist in our relationship color my feelings for her. I refused to let her butter me up. I had to keep my distance. Allowing her to get close could only hurt me down the road.

When Carolyn rang the doorbell, Mother greeted her as if she hadn't seen the girl in 20 years. "Why, Carolyn, good to see you. Come in, dear. How are you? I haven't seen you for awhile."

"I was here just the other day, Mrs. Gaston. And you drove carpool this morning. Don't you remember? That was me in your backseat."

Mother pretended not to hear her.

Carolyn and I closed ourselves in my room and spent the evening talking about Donny Sneed, Marty Morris and the new kid in Mrs. Weaver's class. We sang and danced to music blasted from my new 8-track tape player. We read *Tiger Beat* magazines and an old *Cosmopolitan* I had smuggled from beneath Mother's bed. Mother, Daddy and Oma watched TV in the living room and Mother never once banged on the wall for us to turn the music down—another miracle I chalked up to Oma.

I either ignored or deflected Carolyn's questions about how things were going since Oma moved in. I didn't want to talk about it. I was too confused by it all. Carolyn got mad and sulked for awhile because I "wasn't any fun anymore" and was "acting like a little snit." She was right, of course, but I didn't care.

At 10 o'clock, I heard Daddy go to bed, and a few minutes later Mother said "good night" through my door. The sliver of light from beneath it disappeared shortly after that. Carolyn and I stayed up awhile longer, but my "pissy attitude," as she called it, had ruined the evening and she was soon ready for lights out.

"So, your grandmother is really going to sleep on the couch, huh?" Carolyn asked through the darkness, climbing over me to sleep next to the wall. It was a tight squeeze. She didn't like the old lady look of Oma's bed and had refused to sleep in it. Gave her the creeps, she said. But I realized quickly that either I'd have to move to Oma's bed or I'd have to sleep on the floor. Twin beds were not meant for more than one body at a time, even ten year-old bodies.

I gave Carolyn time to settle in and nod off, then I eased out from under the covers and approached Oma's bed as if the tatted spread might rise up and stick to me like a spider's web, drawing me in. I couldn't force myself to pull down the covers, but finally perched on the bed's edge, my muscles as rigid as if rigor mortis had already set in.

My hands grasped themselves. With my feet planted in the hardwoods, rooted and unmoving, I realized it was going to be another long night.

At 2 a.m. I sneaked down the hallway and into the living room. Oma had given up on the couch. Who could blame her? It was as hard as cinderblock and its fabric was almost as rough. I found her stretched out in Daddy's Naugahyde recliner with an antique quilt tucked clear up under her chin as if the dead of winter had paid us a return visit in May. The J.C. Penney comforter was nowhere in sight. Mother had probably returned it—she called herself frugal; I called her cheap. Oma's bare legs were left exposed to the chill of window unit air. Her chenille slippers dangled from feet splayed toward opposite poles.

I thought about readjusting the quilt for her, repositioning it so it covered her better, or even going back to my room to fetch another blanket that would keep her warm. I thought about waking her and telling her to go get into bed, that I couldn't sleep and there was no need for her to stay out here when she could be more comfortable in bed. I even considered waking her to apologize. Yes, seeing her all rumpled and contorted in what I knew was the most uncomfortable chair known to man, I felt bad for her, and even worse about myself. I realized for the first time that I was a spoiled brat, selfish and despicable, and that this woman did not deserve the misery my mother and I had dumped upon her.

But, of course, I did none of these.

Instead, I folded myself into a tiny ball in a straight-backed chair across the room. With my knees tucked under my nightgown, I wrapped my arms around myself and watched my grandmother sleep. I counted her breaths. I wondered about her dreams. I whispered questions to her about her life, her marriage, the birth of my mother, what Mother's childhood had been like, where they had lived, what Mother had liked to do as a child. I didn't know about other things to ask, like why she had abandoned her family when my mother was my age, only to return months later like nothing had happened. It would be years too late before I would know to ask those things. Oma didn't hear my whispers. She never stirred or even twitched. Oh, she snored, of course, loudly and with gusto. But she had no knowledge of the intimate time we shared in the chilled dimness of our tiny front room.

I'm not sure when I nodded off, sometime before the sun kissed the dogwood branches outside the picture window on the front of the house. When my crusty eyelids fluttered and pried themselves open around 6 a.m., Oma had vanished. I rubbed by eyes, unsure if she had ever been there. Was she a dream? Was her presence in my life an illusion that would vanish upon waking and leave me shaken and afraid to doze again? I glanced around the room. She no longer slept in Daddy's recliner, but my head now rested on a feather pillow and the quilt that had failed to warm her now encircled my body and was tucked securely around my elbows, hips and toes.

Carolyn had a dentist appointment at 8:30 that morning, so she didn't stay for breakfast. Even if she hadn't had to leave, she probably would have thought up an excuse to do so. I understood. I wanted to escape, too. I half-heartedly apologized for my behavior when I walked her to the door.

"I have a grandmother, too, you know," she said. "Daddy won't let her come to dinner. He's afraid she'll get cozy and never leave." I hugged her neck. Waving goodbye from the car, she yelled, "But we'll spend the night at my house from now on, okay?"

I smiled and shut the door.

Daddy had gone into work to finish up inventory, so Mother instructed me to fix myself some cereal. I ate in the living room in front of the TV, but must have dosed off in the middle of *Johnny Quest*. Somewhere between the thick folds of my slumber, a grating noise wrestled me awake. I sat up straight as a yardstick. Mother's familiar whining from the kitchen needled its way through the knotty pine paneling between the two rooms. It was insulin time again. Her litany had one chorus. "Momma, I'm so sorry. I can't. I just can't," and each verse always ended with, "Oh, Lord, I'm going to be sick." I could tell they were still on round one. Mother had probably already tried once to give the injection, failed, and was working up the courage to give it one more go.

I had nodded off with my cereal bowl in my lap. Now, half a cup of 2% homogenized dribbled out and soaked the crotch of my best bell-bottom jeans. I dabbed at the milky liquid with my hand, which did no good, and searched around me for something absorbent to blot up the mess. I found nothing, of course. As much as I hated the thought of it, I would have to cross that threshold, and the recognition of my mission

really pissed me off. It was as if every pent up feeling I'd had since Oma moved in bubbled to the budding surface of my adolescence and crashed into urgency all at once. I jumped up and bounded toward the kitchen. I had taken all I could stand.

Mother looked up when I entered the room, the pink tinge of embarrassment quickly replacing the greenish pallor nausea had colored her in. Her mouth drew up into a knot of chastisement, like it always did before she bellowed, "Nicole Marie, I don't need your help right now. Go to your room." But I didn't give her the chance to speak.

I strode to stand next to her and snatched the syringe out of her hand like I knew what I was doing. I nearly shouted, "Move over," and bumped her out the way with my hip. The expression on Oma's face was a cross between terror and unbridled jubilation. She wasn't the least bit surprised to see me, but she didn't know me well enough to deduce if murder was something I might consider if given half a chance. Even through her uncertainty, the blues of her eyes held the glow of halos, as if her Lord and Savior had just arrived and she was ready to rap upon the door of Paradise if that was His plan.

"I'm probably no better at this than she is," I told her, shrugging toward Mother who was holding up the cabinets again. "But I'm sick to death of listening to her whining day in and day out."

"You'll do fine," Oma said.

I pinched up a hunk of skin too harshly, then readjusted my grip to soften the blow. With an open-mouthed breath of fortification, I inserted the needle with a hand much steadier than I had expected and squeezed the plunger. Then I covered the needle with dry cotton and pulled it out.

Mother still stood shell-shocked by the sink, hanging on to her cabinet life raft, as if the motion of the undulating floor might topple her with the next gust of imaginary wind. Oma reached out and squeezed my hand. She hadn't even covered her eyes.

The world paused for a moment. Nothing more needed to be said or done. I noticed a distant twinkle, a flicker in the blue depths of Oma's eyes that signaled a hope I was not yet willing to allow. "Don't get any ideas," I told her. "There'll be no tatting classes for me."

# Not Your Everyday Cheese Grits

4½ cups milk (yep, NOT water)

1 teaspoon salt

1½ cups quick-cooking grits

2 cups shredded Colby cheese

1 cup shredded garlic cheese (from the deli, not in a plastic tube from the dairy
     section)

1 cup Gruyere cheese (almost too soft to shred, but at least cut it into small
     pieces to assist melting)

¼ cup butter

½ teaspoon white pepper


In a 3-quart saucepan, combine milk and salt; heat up SLOWLY so it is very
hot, but do <u>not</u> let it boil. Gradually stir in grits. Reduce heat. Stir constantly
to avoid scorching, cook 5 minutes. Lower temperature again and add cheeses,
stirring until melted. Stir in butter and pepper.

Some people like to add 3 beaten tempered eggs at this point and to then bake
the grits in the oven. I, however, like them creamy and do not bake mine. I just ladle
them into a bowl and enjoy the cheesy indulgence.

Heaven!!

# Mother's Angel Biscuits

1 pkg. active dry yeast (quick rise)
¼ cup warm water
2 cups buttermilk
5 cups flour
¼ cup sugar
1 tablespoon baking powder
1 teaspoon baking soda
1 teaspoon salt
1 cup lard or shortening, chilled
1 tablespoon melted butter

Have all ingredients at room temperature.

Dissolve yeast in lukewarm water with a pinch of sugar. Set aside for 5 minutes. Stir in the buttermilk, making sure it has first been warmed to room temperature so as not to shock the yeast.

In a mixing bowl, combine flour, sugar, baking powder, baking soda and salt.

Stir all ingredients together to mix well.

Using your fingers—It feels good to get dirty!—work half the chilled shortening into the flour mixture until it resembles coarse meal. Work in the remaining shortening until it resembles large peas.

Stir buttermilk and yeast mixture into the dry ingredients until just blended; do not over mix.

(Continued on next page)

# Mother's Angel Biscuits (continued)

On a clean surface dusted with flour, turn out dough and knead 6 to 8 times, patting together lightly into a flattened circle.

Roll circle out 1/2 to 3/4 inch thick and cut using a floured glass or a 3 inch biscuit cutter. Dip in flour between each cut.

Arrange biscuits on a lightly greased baking sheet; leave 1/3 inch between for softer sided biscuits or 1 inch for more crisp sided biscuits.

Cover with a damp towel or lightly with plastic wrap and allow to rise in a warm, draft-free place until doubled in bulk, or about 45 minutes.

Punch down with 3 knuckles so biscuits will have nice flat tops.

Brush with melted butter before baking.

Bake in a preheated 450 degree oven for 10-12 minutes or until golden brown.

Note: This dough can be refrigerated for 3-5 days, or frozen for up to a month.

# *Prayer*

How many hours have I spent at this keyboard, regurgitating my life and examining it as if each morsel of yesterday's memory holds some clue to my disease of self-doubt? Words spew forth from me in quick bursts of inspiration, only to be scrutinized and discarded as rubbish before my cursory "The End" on the story's last line. Will I ever convince myself that I'm worthy? Will I ever figure out who I am and what purpose my frenetic ramblings have to contribute to this world? And what about teaching? How did I get myself into this? What gave me the idea that I can offer something meaningful to a band of post-pubescent ruffians? Teaching writing and *religion*, no less! Can a teacher inspire confidence if she lacks the quality herself?

I teach my students that God knows what He's doing, that everything happens for a reason, and that trusting in God's Good Judgment will get them through life with a little peace on the side. Physician, heal thyself! Oh, sure, I go through stages of great assurance. When reading my work aloud, even to myself, I recognize the inspiration of the Holy Spirit. I feel the tingle of His fingers across my scalp as the words I've strung together on the screen crystallize into something wondrous that brings tears to my eyes. Is that it? Do I give the credit to God and take none for myself? Is that why I cannot seem to acknowledge my talent? Do I not see it as mine, but rather something handed to me in a gift of reverence, a present dictated through my momentary openness and transmitted through fingers eager to take down each letter, syllable and word?

It is the same with my teaching. I often hold fast to my podium as my students file from the room. I stand breathless and thankful, thinking, "Good Lord, where did all of that come from? I said things I hadn't realized before I said them aloud to my class."

My prayer today is for understanding. May sweet Jesus grant me the strength to accept whatever is given me with a heart primed with self-confidence so each gift, each word, each thought, idea, musing, lesson plan and quote is being delivered to me because I am the perfect person to transmit it. I am God's choice for this mission. I am the only person that can walk this journey and do this job justice. God knows what He's doing.

Lord, help me to shut up and get out of your way.

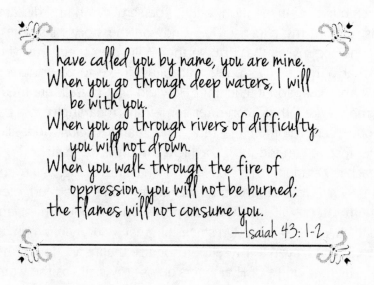

I have called you by name, you are mine.
When you go through deep waters, I will
    be with you.
When you go through rivers of difficulty,
    you will not drown.
When you walk through the fire of
    oppression, you will not be burned;
the flames will not consume you.
                                —Isaiah 43: 1-2

# Fear's Birth

*(Won 1ˢᵗ Place Poetry and was published in* SandScript: A Journal of Contemporary Writing, *Emerald Coast Writers, 2004)*

A wake of exhaust fumes and black smoke
>    lingered long after the National Guard tanks
>    rumbled by our house,
>    its stench so similar to the marchers' torches the night before.
I wondered if Mother
>    would lock us in the bathroom again,
>    if our pillows
>    would be hardened by the porcelain tub,
>    our shoulders
>    stiffened by the tile walls and floor.
I wondered if our dreams
>    would always be tormented by dark figures,
>    our angry friends,
>    seeking justice for the senseless death of their leader,
>    the good Reverend King.
I wondered if fear
>    tastes like the mildewed shower curtain I
>    clinched between my teeth
>    as the fathers of my schoolmates
>    broke every window on the front of our house.

*Julia Schuster*

# *God Screamed Uncle*

From the top bunk, I counted the stars. Stretched out atop the rickety metal structure, crisp sheets fresh from home shielding me from the dust, bed bugs and mattress stains of years gone by, I gazed heavenward through the roof slats, marveling at how much brighter the night sky glowed over the lake than it did over our Memphis neighborhood at home. I wondered, too, how the roof managed to keep the rain out and still afford the grand planetarium effect. "Precision engineering," Daddy always said. But I figured it was, instead, God's way of delivering His grandeur, while allowing us the benefit of not having to sleep in a tent anymore. God was good in those ways. He wanted us to enjoy the great outdoors that Daddy was determined for us to experience, but God knew that I was not too fond of cot sleeping, mosquito bites and the fear of a copperhead or Pygmy rattler joining us in the middle of the night.

The Well House, as we called it, rested precariously on stacked cinderblocks on a high spot along the shore of Pickwick Lake. I suppose it got its name from the smelly well in the front yard. Even though no one I knew was brave enough to draw water from it, I liked the wooden bucket, frayed rope and metal hand crank, all sheltered under the little pitched roof. It reminded me of a wishing well in a story Mother had read to me as a younger child. The children in the story made wishes, their eyes closed tightly to give their wishes more "umph." They believed that the well held great magic, enough to make their dreams come true. I never let John or Arthur see me doing it, but on busy afternoons when everyone else was taking a dip in the lake, I'd sneak back up to the house and toss my own wishes the well's way. I would crank down the bucket, leaning ever-so carefully over the rim of the well to hear the splash as it hit water, and I'd whisper my desires down upon it, knowing they would only come true if the rope and bucket carried them all the way to the water at the center of the earth. I wished for good grades so Mother would be happy and proud of me, for longer vacations because Daddy was more fun at the lake than he was at home, and that John and Arthur would join the circus and move away so I'd be an only child and they could not torment me anymore. I never really meant that kind of wish, though, but figured that all sisters wished their brothers would disappear for awhile every now and then. Plus, the circus would have been a fun place for them. I never wished death or disease or rotten teeth on them. That would have been "cruel and unusual," as Daddy always said.

One weekend when I was nine, a great cloud puffed up over the treetops. Its color began as a soft kitten gray, but swirled, within minutes it seemed, into a molten blackness usually reserved for horror flicks. The calm surface of the lake reacted in unison with the clouds. Waves grew from ripples to mounds to whitecaps and lapped at the hull of our ski boat, tossing it about and causing its ropes to grow taut against the splintered wooden dock. Daddy waded chest deep into the water and struggled to free the lines, while Mother rushed around like a headless chicken, clucking and shooing us toward the house as we all snatched up tuna sandwiches and potato chips newly freed by the wind.

The new Barbie beach towel Mother had bought me with some of her grocery money fluttered up like a butterfly testing its wings for the first time. The wind billowed under it, taking it higher and higher into the air.

I heard Mother yelling, "Elisa May, get in the ditch. Get into the ditch," but chasing my beautiful towel had engrossed me. The storm and its danger had become less threatening than losing my towel. Leaves kicked up all around me. Small branches slapped my ankles. Dull echoes of shouts from my brothers and the high pitch screams of my frantic mother ebbed and flowed in my consciousness as if shouted into a tin can. They did not spur me into action as my legs and raised hands took me further and further away from the safety of the house and its wishing well.

A crooked limb of an ancient oak tree nabbed my towel and unfurled it like a flag raised to half-mast in remembrance of a fallen soldier in the war. I sprang from a flatfooted stance on bare feet to try and catch it, but the wind teased me each time, keeping it just out of reach. By now the rain had started, pelting my sunburned shoulders and causing my ringlets to flatten into drenched ribbons against my face. The flapping towel mesmerized me and held me there, transfixed on my mission and unconscious of the swirling bedlam taking place all around me. I knew nothing else . . . until I heard the crack.

Every sound in the universe joined forces to deliver the effect, all thunder, all echo, every drum, explosion, car wreck and bomb. The ground vibrated like the fist of Satan had slammed hard into mankind and God had screamed, "Uncle!" to let the devil know he had won. The top branches of the great oak ripped like fine linen in a game of tug of war, and I watched the massive trunk succumb to the blow as if the devil's fiery three-pronged spear had split it in two. The light show rivaled all Fourth of July celebrations I'd ever known. Red, white and blue sparkles danced against a backdrop of solid black. I don't remember it ending, though. I don't recall the grand finale, or singing the *Star Spangled Banner*, or hot dogs with pickle relish, or cotton candy, or the marching band.

From the top bunk, I count the stars. Stretched out atop the rickety metal structure, crisp sheets fresh from home shielding me from the dust, bed bugs and mattress stains of years gone by, I gaze heavenward again through the roof slats, marveling at how much brighter the night sky glows over the lake than it does over our Memphis neighborhood at home. I lift my hand to my face. It feels funny. Is that the smell of scorched squirrel tail lingering too close to my nose? Or something else?

"Oh, thank God." My mother's cool fingers stroke my brow. "She's coming around. Elisa May, it's me, it's Mother. Can you hear me? Dear Lord, let her be okay."

My eyelids flutter, although I know they are open. The pink haze around me diminishes. I move my lips, but no words escape. All I see is the Big Dipper. As close as my mother, the stars beckon and I want to join them up there. I remember a wish I made last summer that I'd grow up to become an astronaut, that I'd travel by spaceship into heaven, that I'd walk on Venus and visit the planet where all the angels live. I don't want to leave, though, not now, not yet. I don't want to go off to a star-cast circus. I'd miss John and Arthur. I'd miss Mother and Daddy. I'd miss the half-eaten tuna fish sandwich and secretly tossing my wishes down the wishing well. A tingle begins in my fingers. It tiptoes up my tanned arms and lingers like a ballerina on point at the base of my neck. The Twins of Gemini reach down to me, their sparkling hands so appealing. I blink twice, rise up through the roof slats, and join them, saying farewell to my summer at the Well House.

# Mother's Tuna Salad

1 large can Albacore white tuna, shredded with fork to desired mushiness
2 large dollops of Miracle Whip salad dressing
1 large dollop of sweet pickle relish <u>plus</u> a dribble or two of the relish juice
salt and pepper to taste

Mix all ingredients well.

To serve: Smear 2 large slices of your favorite bread with Miracle Whip. Apply a huge portion of tuna salad to bread. Add fresh sliced Ripley tomatoes and lettuce leaves. Top with other slice of bread and enjoy!

<u>Side note:</u> Mother never heard of Albacore tuna—she only used Chicken of the Sea packed in oil—but evolution is a wonderful thing. I grew up eating my "tuna fish salad," as we called it, on pasty Colonial White Bread, but maturity has introduced me to the finer white breads found in good bakeries, such as crusty French, Farmer's Bread, Sourdough, etc. I still don't believe God meant for tuna fish salad to be eaten on wheat bread, but if you like it that way, go for it, honey. Just don't make me watch!

# *Fruitcake Cookies and Bringing Mother Back to Life*

*(Published as "Ah, Fruitcake!" in* A Cup of Comfort for Sisters, *Adams Media, 2003)*

I stood at my sister's kitchen counter chopping pecans while she rifled through the cabinets between my legs in search of her industrial-sized baking sheets.

"Oh, this will be such fun," she chattered, "baking fruitcake cookies with you for the first time in all these years."

I spread my legs a little wider and looked down at her. "What do you mean fruitcake cookies? These pecans are for my famous cocoon cookies. I hate fruitcake."

If I had been a man I would have been castrated with one sharp blow. Her head came up so fast and with such force I barely had time to step back and get out of the way. She turned to face me. Her mouth gaped and her hands agitated the air from her position in the floor. "Hush, hush your mouth. It's a sacrilege against everything good and holy to say

> Exaggeration is the inseparable companion of greatness.
> —Voltaire

such a thing. Baking fruitcake cookies the week before Thanksgiving is a family tradition. We will do it, and we will do it with the respect our fore-mothers set down for us all those years ago."

I couldn't respond for a few moments. I stood there with my butcher knife still poised in mid-air. Finally I said, "What planet are you from? I've never made fruitcake cookies. And whose tradition? Our mother never had a tradition that included any kind of chunky cookie with disgusting lumps of candied fruit. We made cocoons, cookie press cookies, Daddy's favorite oatmeal chocolate chip with red and green M&Ms to make them festive, and of course, cut-outs with Mother's butter cream on top. Nowhere does candied fruit figure into my family recipes."

Sissie's palm caught her scream. She bowed to the ground, almost weeping, like a female Dali Llama doing penance for a horrible sin. She whispered, "Mother failed you, pure and simple. I got married too young and left you to be raised by a menopausal wreck. She had me as a child, and you as an old hag."

"What are you talking about?"

"This, just this. You are my little sister and all you know about tradition is cookie press cookies and oatmeal chocolate chips. What else did she fail to teach you? Do you have good dental hygiene? Do you have a clue how to bake bread? How many pickles do you put up each year? Did you breast feed Mary Kate or was she a bottle baby? Oh, Lord, help me, I think I might fall out right here."

"I turned out just fine, I'll have you know," I sat back. "I don't know what you are talking about. The only pickles my mother ever put up were Claussen's. They came from the refrigerated aisle at Kroger and they lived in our refrigerator, the middle shelf on the door. Wonder Bread contributed to these hips and Mary Kate did beautifully on Enfamil, thank you very much."

I then worried if she might have been serious about the fainting part. The parenthesis around her mouth turned chalky and her eyes began to float in their sockets like tiny bars of Ivory soap. I extended my hand to my overly dramatic sibling and helped her to her feet, realizing all the while that our living apart for so long had warped our sense of each other. She described family cooking traits and experiences that I had never known. How could that be? Was she going through some kind of emotional breakdown? Maybe my moving so close by after so many years of living away had traumatized her in some way. I led her over to the kitchen table and eased her into a chair. "It's okay," I said, patting her hand. "I'd love to learn how to make fruitcake cookies and I guess the reason I'm here is so you can teach me how."

She looked into my face, studying my infant crow's feet as if she had never seen me before. "Cornbread, you certainly know how to make cornbread. Tell me you do."

"Jiffy Muffin Mix," I whispered, feeling suddenly inadequate and out of sorts.

"Pound cake. Oh, tell me you know how to make pound cake."

"Duncan Hines," I replied.

"Spaghetti sauce?" Her eyes started to tear.

"Prego Traditional with mushrooms. It's good, honest it is."

"Please don't tell me you buy chicken stock in a can." A moan escaped her.

I could no longer admit the truth.

"Oh, Lordy. I'll have to start from scratch. But I've already raised my family. Hugh and Phillip have put up pepper jelly every year since Allen died. Does this mean I have to start all over again with you?" Her head lolled against the back of her chair, rolling back and forth like a pendulum of regret. She rubbed her face with arthritic hands; then she sat up straight as a wooden spoon and grabbed my shoulders so I could not escape. "You will learn the traditions of our heritage if I have to hold remedial classes from a nursing home. I will make it my duty that your precious little Mary Kate knows all the secrets of corn chutney and how to assure her angel biscuits are light enough to take flight if need-be. It may be too late for you to perfect the arts, but she is still young. There is hope for her."

Sissie re-fluffed herself.

I decided that it would not be advantageous at this point to put up a fuss. I nodded obediently and resumed my position at the counter with my butcher knife and the other nuts. Sissie dug out the eight pounds of multi-colored candied fruit that she'd had stored in her freezer since ought-one. A slimy night this will be, I thought, stifling the urge to gag.

Sissie took on her culinary duty with a gusto that would make "Just-tone Wil-sone" proud. She instructed me on the proper way to chop our six cups of pecans. I was doing it wrong, of course.

"How many cookies are we making here?" I asked. "Is there any food left for the squirrels to store up?"

"We're making enough to feed the troops at Shiloh, and every living friend and relative our family has claimed since I was born, that is except for Uncle Fred on Daddy's side. Bill Ennis takes a dozen to his great-grand-momma's grave instead of flowers each year, you know.

People are depending on us, so start chopping or we'll be here all night."

"And people really eat these things?" I asked. "I mean, they don't use them as skeet or doorstops or anything like that, do they?"

I ducked as her hand whizzed past my head.

She snatched a spoon from my hand at one point. "Just get your hands in there, Miss Smarty Pants, but be gentle. We don't want to wound the dough." Then she explained how to assure that our cookies had just the right amount of liquor to make them tasty but not so much that anyone would get soused.

"Liquor?" I said, perking up. With a shot or two of a decent libation, I might survive this night without committing murder, or Hara-kiri on myself.

"Apricot Brandy," she replied, with a dignified nod.

Not my favorite, but at that point I would take anything I could get. At first she refused the offer of a sip, but before long we were both chugging the stuff, as well as licking our intoxicatingly doughy fingers. Our ornery chatter finally mellowed into giggles, which erupted without provocation and had us weeping and almost wetting ourselves.

When we recovered, I said, "I wish Mother had taught me these things. Maybe I would like fruitcake cookies if I had been introduced to them early on."

"Oh, you *will* like fruitcake cookies before this night is done," Sissie said, "But, I regret that we can't nip this whole cooking problem in the bud. If only I had Mother's recipe box. I could teach you every livin' thing you ever wanted to know. Gee, I wonder whatever happened to it? I guess Daddy sold it in the garage sale when he and his new hussy moved into their fancy new motor home. Ain't that just our luck?"

"You mean that old green tin box?" I asked. "The one stuffed with all those magazine recipes and scraps from yellow note pads?"

"That's the one."

Our eyes met. She knew what I was about to say, and it took everything she could do to keep from exploding into squeals before I got the words out.

"It's in my kitchen, in the cabinet over my stove," I announced.

The next thing she saw was my backside. My feet were out the door and hoofing it down the street. I was back in record time, panting and holding the green tin box with all the reverence of the Holy Grail. I placed it on the counter in front of us, which Sissie had wiped clean in preparation of its arrival in her home. I let her do the honors of lifting the lid. We gazed at the crumpled papers and note cards living within it as if we were looking into the womb of the Holy of Holies. Sissie fingered the edges of our Mother's lifetime and paused reverently before grasping one piece between her finger and thumb. She gave a tug.

Mary Horst's *Fresh Coconut Cake*. (That's our mother)

We both "aah'ed" and tears welled up again. I removed the next jewel.

Aunt Bill's *Fresh Apple Cake*.

We took turns ushering each recipe out of its tomb with all the fanfare we could muster without falling completely apart. Aunt Willard's *Angel Biscuits, Company Peas*. We blinked convulsively to clear our view. Francis Stovall's *To Die For Cheese Cake*, Paula Ennis' *Cranberry Orange Salad*, Daddy's Favorite *Shit on a Shingle, Eggs a la King*—no one claimed it—and Granny's *Homemade Peach Ice Cream*.

Our mother was right there with us. We could taste and smell each delicacy as we removed it lovingly from the box. We read the titles aloud in a kind of litany to our family heritage and to the mother we were certain was sitting across the kitchen table from us at that very minute. Sissie pulled a recipe and recited a memory to go with it.

By the time we had emptied our green memory tin, it was 4 a.m. We had sobered up and twenty-four dozen fruitcake cookies had been cooled, tinned, Christmas-bowed and put away. Most importantly, we had revived a family tradition that will last for generations to come. Now, the week before Thanksgiving, we bake fruitcake cookies with my daughter—the same way Sissie did in her youth and the way I did vicariously through the rich stories she shared with me that night. And we always clear off a place at the kitchen table for Mother. You see, I didn't miss out on anything growing up. No, I'm the little sister who has everything a little sister, and a daughter, could ever want or need—a mother whose legacy is alive and well, and a sister who loves me enough to teach me how to make cookies I despise.

> Fruitcake cookies' only saving grace, besides the brandy, has got to be the pecans. Called "the lucky nut," pecans are said to bring prosperity.

# Mrs. Paula Ennis' Fruitcake Cookies

6 cups chopped pecans
1 lb. white raisins
1 - 8 oz. package dates
1 lb. candied cherries
1 lb. candied pineapple
¾ cup flour (to mix with fruit)
1 stick oleo
1½ cups light brown sugar, packed
4 large eggs
2¼ cups flour
3 scant teaspoons soda
½ teaspoon cinnamon
1 teaspoon nutmeg
½ teaspoon cloves
5 tablespoons milk
½ cup apricot brandy

Chop nuts and fruit well, then flour fruit and nuts with the ¾ cup of flour. Set aside. Cream oleo and brown sugar well, then add eggs one at a time, beating well after each one. Sift dry ingredients, and add sugar mixture. Add milk and brandy. Add to this mixture the nuts and fruit and mix well.

Drop by tablespoons full onto lightly greased cookie sheet. Bake at 325 degrees for 12 to 15 minutes.

Note: Sissie often doubles this recipe. I, on the other hand, avoid it at all costs.

# Funeral for a King

I stood knee-deep in a weeping sea of funeral flowers, the skeletal fingers of dying lilies and bruised spider mums groping at me in the mid-August heat. He had already been dead three days, the service not planned until Sunday, but his throng of twenty thousand mourners would not leave this place. Their sweaty grief hung heavy, low atop the ground, wafting in through the iron gate bars that kept them at bay. It choked me, its stench, with smelly hands around my throat stronger than the wilting botanical arrangements their grief had offered up to their King. Hundreds pleaded with me through the bars of their outdoor prison, "Let us in, please, let us in." I thanked God for our corrupt police force, and ignored the mourners as best I could.

The three-day old parade of flower shop vans continued, rolled up, one by one, stopping, doors flung open before tires had a chance to stop. I let the hired help unload each offering, then directed the careful placement of thousand dollar funeral sprays and twenty-dollar bud vases, as if they were the same. I carefully removed each card and personal sentiment until my apron pockets bulged and I leaned forward slightly with their weight, before pouring, drop by drop, each arrangement into the putrid wave of flora that flowed north toward the mausoleum at the top of the hill.

No one believed that they'd bury him here, let alone house his coffin in a concrete tomb above the ground. Surely someone would steal his body, sell it at auction to the highest bidder, or mummify it so the whole world could gawk at him for the rest of time. Speculation ran rampant and fueled the fervor of his fan base. They felt an obligation to stay forever, keeping watch to make sure no more harm came to their beloved King. They'd move him, wouldn't they? Place him somewhere safer, somewhere secret, somewhere more fit for the status he'd achieved? But no, he'd specified Forest Lawn, in a golden crypt close to his momma, Gladys Presley, who had already rested there, unharmed, for quite some time.

One of Daddy's shop vans pulled up. I moved toward it, hoping my brother might be driving, come to relieve me, save me from the madness, the heat. Bees drunk with anticipation of pollen soon angered at its absence. They didn't realize that florists and decapitation from Mother Earth's source sterilizes flowers, dries up their tiny breasts and renders them unfit to feed. When I got close enough to the van to see the driver, it was a delivery boy, not my brother, who hopped out to unload. He struggled with a large bouquet. I should have run to help him; instead, I watched in a kind of shocked pause as Liberace's spray, my mother's creation, tilted and swayed. It was a white rose grand piano, complete with silver candelabra, and fashioned out of five full sheets of Styrofoam, ten dozen white roses, hundreds of pink carnations and held together with enough duct tape to build a small car. It teetered on the brink of disaster for one moment, two; then it took flight. My mother had taken the order over the phone, wrote each digit of Liberace's credit card number by hand, and taken dictation of his sympathy, word for word. She thought it might be fun to keep the yellow copy of all the famous people's credit card slips, skewer them to a bulletin board in the showroom to illustrate to our regulars that celebrities made Sander's Florist their choice on an historic occasion like this.

Daddy said, "Mary, you're just like those crazies. Those lunatics who pay top dollar for one rose, who want us to place it on the ground before he's even in it, then pick up their tacky stem and deliver it their house. They want to keep it forever, they tell me. Have a special *Elvis place* all fixed up in remembrance in their homes. They're gonna worship a damned dead flower, and place it at the feet of Elvis's picture. It's sick, I tell you. We won't lower ourselves to be like them."

As Liberace's offering listed slightly eastward, cracked at its center and rained white petals on the head of our delivery boy who couldn't care less, I wondered if we hadn't already sunk to a level just south of common decency. We'd been proud to decorate Graceland at Christmas each year. At age six, my daddy's "connections" had helped garner an invitation for my whole Brownie troop to eat breakfast out there on his famous Boulevard. Elvis had joined us; he ate four eggs over easy and slopped the yoke up with an angel biscuit light enough to float on air. He'd even given us a tour of the jungle room. Seventeen brown-capped and vested children bored and wishing for a playground. What a tacky place, I remember thinking even then.

Now, looking back almost thirty years, it's clear. Daddy liked the money Elvis living in Memphis afforded us. On his funeral weekend alone we raked in more than three Christmases and two Valentine's combined. What a haul. Daddy was sad about his passing, but not because he cared about Elvis so much. No, he thought the gravy train was over, that our Elvis fan regulars would have no need to tithe with their weekly arrangements to him any longer.

But Daddy didn't yet understand the mindset of obsession.

Nothing much has changed. We still deliver those standing orders of birthday and anniversary wishes. His fans never missed a beat.

I wonder, though: Does anyone mark the day he popped his first pill?

No, the whole world believes — Elvis Lives!

# Ants Gotta Bite,
# Sun Gotta Burn

*(Published in* On Grandma's Porch, *BelleBooks, 2008)*

Queen Esther Ashcraft Gaston was my grandmother's name, and she lived up to its loftiness, certainly not in wealth or social stature, but in the richness she passed down to her wisdomless clan. I fancied her a royal, but she was far from stuck on herself. She was genteel and kind, with a unique way of humbling herself to mingle with us "relative" commoners who needed someone to teach us what was what.

My family always visited her in the summertime, usually during the month of July, when the humidity in Deland, Florida was at its peak and could suck streams of perspiration out of you, drenching your shirt and under-drawers in nothing flat. I remember those visits as some of the happiest days of my young life. All except one summer, that is.

Oh, I must have been about five or six years old. Our pea green, 1959 Chevrolet Impala Estate station wagon crunched along the shell road toward Granny's house. We'd been driving since midnight. I couldn't wait to get out of the car, and away from my brothers—John, who relished tormenting his baby sister to the point of making me scream or tickling me to the point of wetting my pants. And Arthur, who had just reached puberty and had not yet learned the advantages of deodorant. Once a week did not cut it, and ninety-five degree heat only made the fumes rise faster to my nose. The boys hogged the back seat—me sandwiched me in the middle and never allowed to "claim" the window seat. How did our parents ever survive those trips without

Nintendo, DVDs or at the very least, CDs or cassettes? Better yet, how did I ever survive them?

Before our tires came to a complete stop in front of Granny's house, I vaulted John and forced open the car door, eager to escape the stale air. I jumped out with sandaled feet, and without noticing *the mound*. It took a few seconds for my travel-numb limbs to react to the bites, but when the pain hit, my siren wailed. A regiment of tiny red soldiers charged up my legs and into my shorts. They covered my lower extremities in a matter of seconds, even got into my panties. My white

flesh turned angry red and fluid with six-legged poison machines. I howled. I kicked, goose-stepping, and squealed, searching around frantically for something to rub up against. With me dashing about like a Comanche meeting the warpath head-on, Mother had a dickens of a time catching me after she clambered from the car. She slapped at my legs with her headscarf. Daddy cursed. Even John and Arthur chipped in to beat off the little buggers. I'd never been so happy for a whipping. But fire ants fight to the death. They were not giving up.

By the time Granny heard the ruckus and made her way from out back near the fern-packing shed to the front porch, I had hundreds of bites from my waist to my feet. Granny snatched me up and dashed to the side of the house where she dropped me into the rain barrel, pushing my head below the surface with great force. Green algae choked me and got sucked up my nose. But when I came up, gasping, I was thankful and certain that my queen had saved me from a horrible death.

"Just sit right there and let the water soothe you," she said. "I'll fetch the salve, and I'll be right back."

She disappeared around back of the house, unfazed and unruffled. I wondered how she had managed to remain so calm. Royal blood, I figured. She hadn't screamed, "Lord, have mercy, my baby, my baby," like Mother had. She had just acted, swiftly and with total control of her senses. I had known and loved this woman my whole life, but only then did I realize she was a woman to be admired.

I did okay for a few seconds, just bobbing there in the barrel, the water cool on my burning legs. Then I realized that I was alone on the side of a house so eerie and mysterious it took me weeks to overcome the nightmares that always followed me home. It didn't exactly resemble a castle. A rundown old Florida homestead was more like it, sitting on cinder blocks and listing slightly to the left. Live oaks dripping with Spanish moss domed the property. Their shadowy crown added a horror flick atmosphere that fueled the imagination of this grandchild ripe for suspense. Their shade was essential for Granny's Plumosus fern business, but to me the gloom concealed monsters that lurked under the blades, waiting to jump out at the next passerby or the next child left alone in a rain barrel.

I screamed.

Where had the rest of my family gone? Had they all been attacked by the biting varmints? Were they out front in a battle with the tiny foe? Or what if . . . what if . . . what if the fern monsters had gotten them and eaten them all up? "Aheeeeee!" Finally my mother's voice came to me from someplace above. I looked up and found her. She stood on the screened porch, her face pressed against the mesh.

"Oh, baby girl, are you okay? I'd come down there but those critters are everywhere. This place is crawling with them, just like it always was when I was a child."

"I want out," I wailed.

My mother was scared out of her wits. I could tell by the way she scanned the ground around me. I could tell by the way her hands rubbed her arms as if she were cold. What other reason could keep her away from me in my time of need? I had never witnessed her in such a state. It caused me to pause in my pain and wonder how itsy-bitsy red bugs could wield the power to cause such a horrible thing—a mother paralyzed with fear.

But fear is contagious. I caught it and quaked.

"I can't get out. I want out. I want out NOW! It hurts, Mother, it hurts soooooo bad." Tears rolled as my agony recharged. Green slime and imaginary water beasts threatened to gag me again.

"It's okay, doodle bug, just hold on. Granny will be right back with the salve, quick as a minute. She's immune to those dad-blamed creatures. They gave up on her long ago. But she'll fix you up like she always did me."

Thankfully, Mother was right. Granny reappeared and lifted me from the muck. And for a woman of close to eighty, she was one strong broad. But now, slime dripping from my toes was the least of my worries. The air hit my bites like a thousand needles. I started yelling and I didn't quit until the Paregoric kicked in.

The next few days remain a blur to me. I guess doping me out of my mind was easier than listening to me lament like a captive damsel in distress. When I finally recovered, I had major catching up to do. My brothers had already been to Silver Springs to ride the glass bottom boat, see the mermaids, and marvel at the human pyramids of championship water skiers who dazzled the crowds there seven days a week. Plus, they'd been down the St. John's River fishing with Uncle John A. I had missed out on everything. This vacation was from hell. I was cranky and bite pimpled and it was time for high-style Julia pampering. I deserved better than this.

When Daddy carried me to the car, (because I refused to place my feet anywhere near the ground) I sported a pity-party attitude that I was certain would gain me extra trinkets at the local souvenir store. Boy, was I wrong. Granny didn't react kindly to emotional blackmail. I was lucky to get to go to the beach, or so I thought.

Daddy drove and Granny rode shotgun. "Daytona, here we come!" Granny rattled off directions, pointing left, and then right while I sat in amazement in my usual spot in the middle of the back seat. This was a curious thing, I thought, a first in my five-year-old history. No one had ever told my daddy where to go. But there he sat in the driver's seat, quietly following Queen Esther's commandments, and never raising his bushy left eyebrow or grumbling under his mustache.

Normally, I thought of Granny as a vanilla woman, who wore only regal shades of gray, beige and white. She had Clorox-white hair, braided and coiled into a crown on top of her head, as cottony soft as my pillowcase. I recall her as if she were perpetually seated in a black and white photo, even when she was right there before me in the flesh, with gray shades being the boldest her personality could muster up. But here, in her domain, Granny took on an air of authority that she could have never pulled off in Memphis on her visits to see us. She spoke and everyone listened. With words delivered with a smile and in a quieter-than-normal tone, her meaning came across with clarity and kid glove force.

At the beach she said, "Julia Elisa, come here and let me slather on this here Coppertone." I wrinkled up my nose, but obeyed. "Yur' momma and John A. will be comin' to git me real soon. I can't stay out here with y'all an' bake all day. I got work to git done under those hammocks. Those ferns gotta be cut, packed an' shipped today. But you mind my words, now, youngin'—in a little while yur' to put on this here shirt yur' daddy brought, and sit here underneath this umbrella so'ens you don't get scorched. Don't forget, now, or those bites will come back to life and have you ruby red and wailing all over again."

"Yes, ma'am," I replied, taking no mind.

By bedtime the blisters rose. My shoulders puffed up with a septic ocean boiling just below the skin. Hot red—I couldn't sit, I couldn't stand and I certainly could not lie down. There was no position of comfort, no salve that could ease the pain. Granny cut five stalks from the aloe vera plant, gelled me up good and prayed to the Lord Almighty that I'd get some relief. Then it was once again time to bring on the dope. Mixed with peanut butter to kill the taste, Mother spooned Paregoric down me and before long oblivion took me to a place of tormented dreams, fern monsters and fire ants bigger than the flying monkeys in the *Wizard of Oz.*

The next morning as I awakened from sitting straight up all night on my cot in the corner of the dining room, I overheard my brothers discussing how Daddy had just stood there and taken it when Granny reamed him up one wall and down the other for not watching out to make sure I didn't get char-broiled. First taking directions, and now a good reaming out? This woman, Queen Esther Granny, must have some kind of power to accomplish all of that in these few short days, I thought.

A few more miserable days of healing passed. They seemed to go on forever. I was not a happy camper, but I knew better than to bitch and moan too much. I was bored out of my mind, but reluctant to leave the house. It seemed that the out of doors that had once been my playground now held painful dangers that my young years had never experienced before. I started to understand why my mother seemed so jumpy. I was more than just jumpy. I was ready to bolt.

Arthur came into the kitchen one afternoon in search of some needle-nosed pliers to fix his fishing line. I was helping Granny make fried chicken for dinner. It had taken all I could muster to stand on the back porch and watch her swing that poor bird by the neck till it was dead. I was a city girl. I had never seen anything so tragic. Now, I stood across the room while she chopped the creature to bits. My stomach churned just a little, but I managed to choke it down.

I guess she figured a little cooking would keep me occupied since I had run out of things to play with and had refused to set foot off the porch for fear of another ant attack. After all, those little varmints knew I was there and that I tasted good. They were sure to come back for a second course of me. Granny's hands were caked with flour, so she pointed Arthur and me to search through some of her less-used kitchen junk drawers for the pliers. I was glad for the distraction. I rummaged through a couple, and then came upon one with a stubborn attitude that was hidden behind the entry hall door that never got shut. I tugged hard, leaning into it. I tugged once, tugged again. When it finally gave way, it gave way with gusto. It flew open, tossing me onto my rump on the floor and something black and hairy into my lap. The beast scampered across my belly, ran up my arm, and around my tender shoulders before scurrying off in a mad dash to escape human wrath. Screaming at a pitch that would break Hobnail glass, I leaped into my brother's arms. My fillings quivered.

"Whoa, watch out there," Arthur stuttered, but Granny didn't even pause from dredging chicken parts.

"What's all this commotion about?" she asked calmly.

"It's a rat, or something, Granny," Arthur said, struggling to hold on to me and not let my feet touch the ground. "He's gone now, Julia. It's okay, I won't put you down."

Granny took her time milking and flouring the last breasts and thighs. She placed the pieces on the baking sheet and covered them with a dishtowel before even coming over to see if I had survived. Dusting her hands off on her yellow-checkered apron, she leaned over the drawer, which now lay on the floor, as if investigating a crime scene. "Hum, what have we got here?" she said. "Looks like we got us some good eats for dinner."

Arthur moved a few steps closer, with me hanging around his neck like a talisman of bad luck. That remark had even piqued my interest. Had I heard her right? What on God's green earth could be in a drawer that we'd want for dinner? I wriggled out of my brother's arms, being careful where I stepped, and leaned tentatively over the drawer.

There, eight tiny rat-lings lay nestled in with the canning tongs and Mason jar lids. Their eyes weren't even open yet. They squirmed close to each other, searching their dishrag nest for the mother they knew had been there just moments ago.

My hand caught the first droplets of vomit. No way was I eating baby rats. I ran out the back door toward the outhouse, and under the arbor of four o'clocks, but I only made it as far as the packinghouse stoop. When I returned, still green and queasy, I slumped into a vinyl kitchen chair. Granny was just lifting the first few chicken legs from the hot oil.

"We're not really eating those little critters for dinner, are we, Granny?"

She didn't answer. She just raised her eyes to me and smiled one of those smiles that are impossible to decipher. "Did any ants attack you on your way to the john?" she asked.

I thought for a minute. "No, ma'am."

"Any other catastrophe besiege you? Wasps, hornets, yellow flies?"

"No, Ma'am."

"A fern monster grab your leg while you upchucked?"

I shook my head.

"So I guess you're gonna help me wash the fronds tomorrow and get them packed, iced and ready to ship off to florists all across these fine United States then?"

The snakes my mother had mentioned that slither amongst the ferns and often visit the packinghouse came to mind. I had to pause before answering. Could I really do it? Could I handle being out there with danger lurking at my feet, just waiting to bite me, burn me, or jump into my lap? I wasn't sure.

"Your momma is a wonderful woman, but I did her wrong raising her up. I coddled her to the point of making her wimpy. It's my fault, not hers. I didn't want my baby to suffer. I didn't want her to have to deal with pain and strife. But it don't have to be like that, ya' know. You're a strong little dickens. Just look how you handled yourself with those pesky old ants. And I've never seen a child brave a sunburn like you got as well as you did. This here is a prime opportunity to face those big bad monsters you've created for yourself. Them ants gotta bite and that sun gotta burn, but you, youngin', gotta snub your nose at it all. You can either be a shrinking violet or stand tall like a hardy mum. It's yur' pick."

> It is a cheery thought to think that God is on the side of the best digestion.
>
> —Donald Robert Marquis, from: 'archy does his part'

Granny turned back to tend her chicken.

I sat there for a long while. I traced the flower pattern on the vinyl tablecloth with my finger, not having the courage yet to answer or to join Granny at the stove. Finally I moved to stand beside her. I tugged on her apron. She stopped and looked down.

"How do you keep those ants from biting you, Granny?" I asked.

She tussled my hair. "Meanness, for one thing, pure meanness. They know better than to mess with Queen Esther Ashcraft Gaston. I can be as mean as a snake, if need be, ya' know. But more than that, youngin', I tread lightly. Yep, I tread lightly and I watch out where I place my feet."

Queen Esther dished up a fine dinner that night, double-coated fried chicken, scrubbed clean potatoes, mashed with homemade butter and fresh milk, lady peas, angel biscuits and tomato slices the size of pancakes. I didn't try the casserole she prepared, though, even after she encouraged me that it was a fine way to snub my nose at my fear. It resembled her cornbread dressing recipe, usually my favorite. But the eight grayish lumps just visible below its crusty surface reminded me too much of baby rats in a drawer.

"What are those?" I asked, pointing to the mounds.

Granny smiled another one of her unreadable smiles.

Daddy scooped a huge helping onto his plate and announced, "Chicken livers, them are chicken livers and gizzards, too. Good ones, I might add. Give 'um a try."

I swallowed hard, and hoped no one ever pulled one over on me like had just been pulled over on him. I wanted so badly to prove to Granny that I was brave, but her fried chicken had been so good, I wanted it to remain in my tummy where it was. Arthur, usually the garbage disposal of the family, didn't indulge in the mystery casserole either. I guess I wasn't the only fearful subject in this kingdom of scaredy cats.

# Queen Esther's Fried Chicken

One fresh chicken, cut up (and I mean really fresh!)**
2-3 cups flour seasoned with black pepper & salt
Big bowl of buttermilk

Kill, scald, pluck, drain and clean chicken, cut into pieces. (Or buy the freshest cut-up bird you can find at your local grocery store.)

Soak pieces in a big bowl of buttermilk overnight.

Fill large, deep cast iron skillet with 2-3 inches of vegetable oil, (Granny used lard) and heat over medium high heat

Dredge buttermilky chicken parts in seasoned flour, then re-dip in buttermilk and dredge again in seasoned flour. Fry in vegetable oil until brown and crispy.

**Please note that Granny never cooked just one chicken. She would "wring" several, and cook enough to feed all the fern grove workers. I have modified this recipe to suit urbanites that like to pretend we know how to cook.

Side note: The chicken has traditionally been a symbol of fertility, but I think of them in a more inspiring way. They must be aware of the darkness, always watching for the slightest hint of light. They honor the dawn and look toward the future, knowing full-well that their futures are likely to be short. Fried, they offer heaven itself to the table.

# Granny's Baby Rat Cornbread Dressing

One pone of cornbread, baked in an iron skillet in the oven, cooled and crumbled.
(Use your grandmother's cornbread recipe—my Granny's is a secret)
10-15 day-old biscuits, cooked and crumbled
These first two ingredients should total about 8-10 cups, give or take a few, and
    according to how hungry you are.
1 huge onion, diced
1 whole stalk of chopped celery—not too thin, not too thick
4-5 cups chicken stock (I use broth from a can, but don't tell Granny. If you
    want the real stuff, see the gumbo recipe in this collection for the perfect
    chicken stock.)
2 eggs
1 teaspoon ground sage
1 tablespoon poultry seasoning
1 stick unsalted butter, melted
8 chicken livers (or dead baby rats, if you're brave enough), boiled with celery tops
    and seasoned to taste.


Sauté onion and celery in butter until tender. Pour chicken stock, eggs, sage and
poultry seasoning into dry ingredients. Add onion and celery. Stir together. Add
salt and pepper to taste.

Transfer into metal baking dishes. Poke chicken livers down into dressing. Pour
more chicken stock over top if it looks too dry.

Bake at 350 degrees for 45 minutes, until golden brown.

# Mourning

I don't have to wonder what it will be like when
you're gone. I already know. You're cold, stiff
and immobile. Lost. I can't find you, can't
talk to you. That you. The one I know
from twenty-five January firsts, the one I know
from showers together when the size, shape and
age of our bodies made no difference, the one I know
from ultrasounds of baby girl heartbeats, heartbeats
that matched our hearts joined, the one I know
from "I believe in One God" for the first time, "the Body
of Christ," and "Amen," the one I know from
tears of joy and sorrow as our loved ones dropped
like too many tulip petals, Katharina,
Fritz, Mary, Otto, Allen, Trey, so
many, many. The one
who could handle the changes and
tragedies life dishes out,
the one I knew I could love through them.
That you.
That you.
The you who cared.

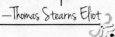

Footfalls echo in the memory
Down the passage which we
did not take
Toward the door we never opened

—Thomas Stearns Eliot

Where is he? You
refuse to remember him, that other you. While
I remember every detail. I search
daily, but he's not here.

And what about the other me, the me
I want back, the me
that hung on as long as I could, that fought
to make you see, but finally gave up, hoping
against hope that the real you would reappear.
The me who enjoyed talking about whatever.
The me that never thought talking was a competitive sport.
The me who never realized that sharing
my ideas about
cooking,
cleaning,
feeding the dog,
grass in the yard,
wall colors,
dust motes,
grocery costs
could be transformed into accusations and
criticism that was never intended, never meant.
The me who could discuss things with
that other you,
talk without accusation,
talk with respect for opinions,
talk with love at its root and
respect as its stem.

## Mourning (continued)

But now, this me, the tired
and giving-up me is
drowning in the frustration of you. I flounder
in the abyss of your missing. The rock
of your anger shatters any hope of my care.
Strike after strike I take
and throw each back with the power of
my pain,
hoping to hurt you,
hoping the force of my ache will
startle you into dawning as these first pink
stripes of daybreak slash the sky,
the wonder and promise grabbing our senses,
rattling our bull-headedness,
shaking us
out of the tortured passage of night,
shaking us
into the lightness of forever.
The promise
The promise
Our vow
that links our hearts and
transforms mourning into peace.

# *The Evolution of the Facts of Life*

*(Published in* Women. Period. *Spinsters, Ink. 2008)*

I sat at the kitchen island with my nine-year-old daughter, watching her slurp angel hair pasta through the most perfect pucker I'd ever seen. Spaghetti sauce droplets joined the freckles that littered the dunes of her cheeks. *She's too young for this,* I thought. *It's too soon.* But I had no choice. I realized that I must tell her the truth and not hedge on the details. It was approaching too quickly for my taste, but better to head off the flood of questions before she filled in the blanks on her own.

My mind floated back to a time in my youth, a time of bubble baths and sponge rollers, go-go boots and David Cassidy. I was nine and a half—not just nine, and not nearly ten, but a full, yet immature, nine and a half. I had played outside all day, climbed into the neighbor's tree house, fought off pirates that looked remarkably like my brothers and painted daisies on the walls of my tool-shed clubhouse—a normal 1967 Spring day.

After a dinner of meatloaf, fried okra and mashed potatoes, Daddy left for the bowling alley to join his team for the league championship. And, as usual, my brothers, John and Arthur, abandoned the kitchen before Mother could include them in clean-up duty. I scraped the dishes while Mother pulled on her rubber gloves and filled the sink with hot water and Palmolive liquid. Seeing her in those yellow gloves made me wish again that Daddy would finally break down and buy her a dishwasher for her birthday. We were the last of our friends to "hold out." It was time. It was way past time.

When Mother cut me loose, I toyed with the idea of going back outside to play—Daylight Savings Time had just started—but instead, I made the girly choice of sinking neck-deep into a humped mountain range of Mr. Bubble suds, while still wondering what my brothers meant when they teased me about taking a bath with a "man." The tub was deep, water warm, air steamy. I scooped up hands full of bubbles to make a beard and mustache, then sat up and constructed puff sleeves and a dress bodice out of the iridescent pink fluff. John knocked on the locked door a few times, yelling for me to hurry up; I ignored him. Arthur was the next to disturb my leisure; I ignored him, too. Being boys, I figured, if they needed to pee they could go outside and find a bush.

When my hands and feet had pickled and the water cooled, I stood up in the tub and splashed myself to rinse off the soapy residue. The coolness trickled down my torso, mingling with the pink bubbles in a river that followed the curves of my flesh. I leaned forward at the waist to wrap my hair in a towel and noticed that the body river darkened to a ghastly red at the top of my inner thighs. My breath caught in my chest as crimson cascaded from some secret place in the vortex between my legs.

The shock stood me upright so quickly that a wave of dizziness washed over me. I grabbed the shower curtain for support. Coughing sounds took no form—*ma, ma, ma, ma, ma*. I danced back and forth in a panic, legs splayed, the water's agitation rocking and sloshing with my distress. My lips formed the word "Mother," but only baby-babble came from the effort. I jerked another towel from the rod and high-stepped onto the tile floor. Red droplets rained down and splashed onto lily-white grout. I threw open the door and dashed out, but in the hallway my wet feet lost traction on the glossy hardwood. I slipped and fell, skidding on my rump into the far wall, a pink imprint of my right hip marring the cream-colored plaster. I scrambled to my feet, towel flying.

When I burst into the den, Mother's shaming look and startled yelp, "What in heaven's name?" alerted me to my nakedness. John and Arthur sniggered as I fumbled with my towel and my face warmed.

"I'm dying!" I finally managed, securing the towel under my armpit. "There's blood . . . blood everywhere. Call an ambulance. I need help!"

No one moved.

A silence usually reserved for hospital waiting rooms or wakes for the dead enveloped the room as a small puddle of pinkness collected around my feet. I reached down and tucked the towel high between my legs, crossing them to keep it there. Mother shot a look of retribution toward my brothers that said, "Leave now or die," and to my amazement they stood and exited by the nearest door, obeying with more haste than I'd ever seen them implement.

"Mother!" I moaned. "Do something, please!"

She rose from her chair with all the urgency of constipation and moved slowly to the telephone table, taking a large arcing route around me as if my plague might be contagious or my illness made me too disgusting to touch. Lifting the receiver, she dialed my sister's number, who was thirteen years my senior, already married and living away from home.

"We need your assistance," Mother said when my sister answered. "It's Julia. She started. I think it would be better coming from you."

I wondered then if my sister also suffered from this horrible ailment. What other reason could there be for "it" to "come from" her? Mother "uh-huh'ed" a couple of times, and "Yes, yes'ed," a few more, then replaced the receiver and turned toward me.

"Get dressed," she said, without inflexion. "Just put an old washrag in your panties until Sissie gets here. She'll bring what you need." She almost looked up at me when she said, "You're awfully young for this, but I guess I should have . . . oh, well, it's too late now." Her eyes glanced instead at the floor, the window, the wrinkles in her hands. Then she walked back to her hysterically floral chair and sat down as if all was well with the world. An *Andy Griffith* rerun was on television. She focused on it, and within seconds she was chuckling with the studio audience, while I stood motionless in the middle of the floor, dripping, my body towel sagging, my hair towel slipping off the left side of my head.

Sissie appeared in my doorway before the *Mayberry* credits ran. I was curled up on my bed in my robe with three bath towels pressed between my legs—just in case the massive abdominal hemorrhage I was experiencing couldn't be contained by a washrag—and wondering why my usually doting mother was now treating me as if I'd farted at one of her Christian Women's Club luncheons. Sissie flew to my side, God love her. Her arms around me had never felt so good. She held me, and didn't say anything until I had cried myself out.

"What's wrong with me," I asked, when the hiccupping sobs subsided. "Am I dying? Do you have this . . . this . . . this illness, too?"

She smiled, but didn't laugh at me. "No, sweetie, you're fine. This is normal. You just started your period. You're a woman now."

I guess the blank expression on my face alerted her to my stupidity. *Period?* How could I start the punctuation at end of a sentence? And what did bleeding profusely have to do with being a woman, I wanted to know. I'd heard rumblings at school about the "womanly mysteries" I would learn about in the "Health" class

> Is solace anywhere more comforting than in the arms of a sister?
> —Alice Walker

I'd have to take in fifth grade, but nothing was mentioned about dribbling blood or washrags in panties. It seemed to me that information that startling would have gotten around. Why hadn't anyone prepared me for this?

"Mother hasn't told you anything, has she?" Sissie asked.

I didn't even know what "anything" she was talking about.

"Oh, good grief," she said, shaking her head as if she were the mother. "I would have thought she'd learned her lesson with me. She's been post-menopausal since you were born, you know. But she didn't warn me either. I was lucky, though. Most of my friends started theirs before me. They clued me in before Mother ever got around to coming clean with the facts."

What on earth was she talking about? Started their what? And what facts? It felt like the female members of my family had been abducted by aliens and now Martians inhabited their bodies and were speaking some language I could not understand. Then, ceremoniously, Sissie presented me with a brown paper bag, recognizable as being from the Rexall drug store near our house. She put such effort into the giving of this odd gift that I was surprised she didn't sing out, "Ta-da," when she placed it in my lap. I peered in, reluctantly, then pulled out a large rectangular box marked "Kotex" and a smaller pink one with "Tampax" written discreetly on the front.

"Don't tell Mother I bought the Tampax," Sissie whispered, cupping her hand around her mouth as if someone might hear. "She thinks they cause cancer, but they are the greatest things ever invented for women. You'll see what I mean."

I opened the cancer-causing Tampax box with two fingers, afraid of what it contained and wondering why my sister would give it to me as a gift, and dumped it onto my bed. But before I could survey its contents, Sissie scooped up the paper-wrapped cylinders. She shielded them with her body as she stuffed them back into the box, as if spies lurking in the shadows of my closet might deduce some top secret biochemical information if she didn't protect it from their unfriendly eyes.

I have to admit that by this point I was beginning to wonder if insanity might run in my family. Sissie ushered me into the bathroom, where she gasped at the blood trail I'd left. Then, stepping gingerly, she ignored it as best she could, locked the door behind us and proceeded to reverently unwrap one of the Tampax cylinders, placing it strategically on the edge of the sink. She then opened the Kotex box and unfurled an inch-thick sheet of what appeared to be Styrofoam with long tails of gauze on each end. Fishing deeper in her bag of contraband, she extracted an elastic contraption with dangling metal barbs.

Suffice to say, my womanly education was a painful experience that took place on the cold, hard, splattered floor tile of our only bathroom. By the time Sissie finished introducing me to a bodily orifice I hadn't known existed, into which we then poked, probed, excavated and embedded a Tampax, and saddled me with the sheet of Styrofoam, looped and tethered with such precision around those metal barbs that she swore would never slip, and I swore this odd flotation devise could keep me afloat indefinitely if the water ever got that high, two hours had passed. Our dear Mother had never darkened the door.

Finally, I kissed Sissie goodbye, but I didn't thank her. I shuffled, bowlegged, back to my bedroom and collapsed onto my bed, sure that I'd never again have the desire to climb into our neighbor's tree house, fight off pirates that looked remarkably like my brothers or paint daisies on the walls of my tool-shed clubhouse. I was certain that life, as I knew it, had ended.

"Mom? Mom, you okay?"

My daughter's words jerked me back to the present.

"Mom, let go. You're crushing my leg."

Ah, the strength of memory, I thought. "Sorry, honey." I patted her leg.

She looked at me with wide nine-year-old eyes. I was sure she was wondering if insanity runs in the family; I knew that look well. Her best friend had showed up at school wearing a bra yesterday. Yes, she was too young for this discussion, but better to know what's coming and not be traumatized needlessly like I had been. After all, once I learned *the facts* and understood them, the knowledge taught me what a miracle this crazy body of mine really is. Of course, not even perpetual therapy had enlightened me as to why some mothers can't bring themselves to talk to their daughters in a loving and open way.

I lifted a corkscrew strand of her golden hair off her cheek and tucked it behind her ear. "How about the two of us go shopping on Saturday, maybe get a bite of lunch, make it a girls' day out?" My fingers lingered in her hair.

"Sure, whatever," she said. "But you're not going to get mushy, are you? I mean, you know how you are." She smiled and I knew she really liked my mushy moments.

"No, I promise. Just thought we needed to spend some time together, maybe buy your first bra. You know, girl stuff."

"Okay, sure, Mom. Whatever."

I decided that I'd better stop by the bookstore before Saturday, or at least Google "The Facts of Life," and do a little research. Things might've changed since the sixties—but then again, nah!

# Unsolicited Opinions about Gift Giving

*(First published in my* Ask a Southern Mother *Newspaper Column for* The Northwest Florida Daily News, *Walton County, Florida)*

I am pleased with myself. I started Christmas shopping before December 23rd this year. The out-of-towner gifts are wrapped and ready to take to the post office. Well, almost all. I even have an idea about what to get my husband. I haven't bought it yet, but I can almost see the outline of it through the fog of uncertainty that shrouds his present every year. It is something he will love, I'm sure, even if it kills me and I'm still shopping for it at closing time on Christmas Eve.

Maybe I've turned my procrastinator's corner, and emerged onto the super highway most efficient people travel everyday. Wouldn't that be a coup?

Like many people, my gift giving practices emerged from the shadow of someone else's. You've all heard about my sister. Her presence and high jinx litter my newspaper column and other writings on a regular basis. She throws the shadow. She is the perfectly-put-together matriarch of my family who *wows* us all with her ability to marathon cook homemade gifts so tasty that recipe requests arrive by mail within days of the gift's receipt. She wraps packages too pretty to open and puts the editors of *Southern Living* to shame with her creative decorating tips. With a sister like mine, it is a wonder I even try.

One thing I've always excelled at is picking gifts that really "fit" the intended recipient. Now, I don't mean "fit" as in "sized properly," although that is a good thing when size is involved. My gifts fit the person's personality. I spend hours researching and scheming, putting out feelers and snooping around homes to figure out what the people on my gift list really want or need and would especially appreciate each year. After all, giving a gift is like giving a part of yourself. The old adage, "It's the thought that counts," is true.

Of course, some people take that to mean that if they think about it, give up and buy something totally inappropriate, it's okay because at least they put the "thought" into it. Wrong!

"Those" people are kind of like those "other" people—gift certificate givers. I am proud to announce to the public at large that I have never once given a gift certificate. Although convenient, pieces of paper (or plastic) with dollar denominations printed on them only demonstrate that the giver doesn't have a clue what the intended receiver would appreciate or like. He or she also doesn't have the good manners to put a little thought into their selection, nor does he or she take the time and effort to do their research.

My mother would have described these people as simply lazy. I conjure up other adjectives to describe them, ones I will avoid using at this time. And whoever invented these paper-stand-ins for presents, forced them upon the general public and convinced many of us to believe advertising over good sense should be horsewhipped.

Gift certificates are my pet peeve, if you can't tell. If you've bought one for me, save yourself the embarrassment. Just substitute someone else's name and give me a warm hug instead.

While I'm ranting about the carelessness of people . . . what is it with those people who buy things no one could sell in a yard sale? Everyone has been the recipient of one of "those" gifts. The kind you open and stare at, wondering, "What the heck is this?" Or you think, "Oh, my God, she'll expect me to display this proudly in my house. Maybe I should just let it slip from my hands now and break so I won't have to carry it home." Of course, you do this all with a sickly grin pasted on your face. Most people have enough manners not to holler, "This is the tackiest thing I've ever seen. What planet are you from?" Well, almost all.

The elderly are the only exception to my rules of appropriate gift giving. Their advanced age and honored place in the grand scheme of the family gains them clemency from being branded "tacky gift giver—avoid at all costs." My grandmother was known to dole out exquisite Staffordshire Cavalier King Charles Spaniel china figurines wrapped in antique hat boxes (both worth a small inheritance), but quickly followed by a plastic-wrapped assortment of sparkly ball point pens with feathered erasers and lured advertisements for tattoo parlors or strip joints. Coming from her, the china figurines exemplified her good taste and the pens demonstrated her never-ending efforts to add a little spice to our otherwise mundane lives.

(I think my daughter even patronized one of the tattoo parlors. They did a fine job on her navel ornamentation. The use of dirty needles or rancid ink didn't even poison her.)

Then there are those gifts that are nice, practical even, but they just don't make any sense. A good friend of mine received one of these gifts recently. She was really glad the giver wasn't present when she opened the box.

Tape, rolls and rolls of tape. Masking tape, Scotch tape, duct tape, emergency medical tape, painter's tape, easy-tear packing tape, high-tack tape, low-tack tape, electrical tape, and a tape dispenser to go with each kind of tape and, of course, a can of adhesive remover for when things got too sticky to handle. I witnessed her confusion. We stood there staring at the assortment, struggling to figure out why anyone would give a person a lifetime supply of every conceivable kind of tape. Was it some kind of joke that she didn't get? Was it something she had done? Did her personality reflect a need for bonding?

We were hard pressed to figure out the riddle. And there must be one. Mustn't there? There was no other explanation that we could deduce.

Then it hit us. The giver must be a tape salesman. He gave tape in an effort to clean out his supply that threatened to take over his tacky life and adhere him permanently to a job he detests. That had to be it.

Phew, I feel better, getting all this off my chest. I wonder, though, which category you fall into? Are you a gift certificate giver? Or are you the giver who makes Martha Stewart's "Good Things" look weak? Do you waste your hard-earned money on gifts that get thrown out with the wrapping? Or are you one of those dear, sweet ancient souls that wraps family heirlooms and plastic party favors in the same box?

My gift giving observations won't hold water with some of you, I'm sure, especially if you find yourself frolicking in the less acceptable categories outlined above. But next time you shop for something special to give someone you love, think about the reason you are giving it. If the effort is just too much for you, and you can't come up with something worthwhile, save your money. Instead, tell the person, eye-to-eye, that you love them and that no bought gift could ever measure up. Tell them in person or in a personal, hand-written letter (not typed out quickly on the computer or in a text message to save time) that your holiday wish for them is happiness, love, and more time to spend with the important people in their lives. After all, Christmas is the season of miracles and peace. No need to add tacky or thoughtless gifts to a blessed season like this.

Dear husband of mine. Did you read this carefully? I can only hope.

# Random Autobiography

I often wonder why
I've only enjoyed snow ice cream
twice in my life, why
the flat moles on my mother's
back appeared on mine
after her death, why
Blondie's puppies had to die in
an ice chest, why
I moved back to Memphis after
escaping it twenty-five years ago.

I often wonder why
I type my grief and failings, why
grass never grew in our Charlotte yard, why
my older daughter is short, why she hates
me, why she chose to call someone else
Mom, why my younger daughter is tall, why she
loves to snuggle, why she asks me questions after
the Ambien has kicked in.
I wonder why my sister is paranoid.

(Continued on next page)

# Random Autobiography (continued)

I often wonder why
it took me so long to figure out
what I wanted to be when I grew up, why
vanilla ice cream tastes best
hand-churned, why my father rarely
hugged me, and only then in quick
pats, never embraces that transmitted heat, and why
my brother carries a 357 Magnun with him at
all times, encased in monogrammed leather, with its
smaller brother tucked inside his tube sock.
I wonder why my brother needs a gun at all?

# No Blind Man's Bluff

I sat on a hysterically floral sofa, across from matching floral chairs and surrounded by massive silk flower arrangements posed on pedestals lining the walls. Light washed into the room from a wall of windows looking out onto the yard. The patio jungle beyond played host to a bounty of greenery and flowering plants. To a less interested party, one might think this room a bereavement chapel in a funeral home. *Musak* played softly in the background. The scent of lilies filled the air. But I knew the truth. My cousin lived here. Betty had grown up like me, in the flower business. Cresting waves of flowers are an intrinsic part of our lives.

I thought for a minute of my home. In recent years, it had lost some of the influences of my father's business. Slowly, one arrangement then another had disappeared from my house, never to return. My front door no longer wore seasonal wreaths that got changed weekly and were stored in translucent plastic bags, which draped the walls of my garage in a perpetual multi-seasonal display from one year to the next. Had I abandoned my heritage, I wondered? By letting go of artificial flora and fauna was I turning my back on my roots?

My guilt lasted only seconds. A profusion of fake flowers can be a tacky way to decorate, especially if it's not done well or with careful attention to decorative function and form.

Betty had done a pretty good job, I thought. A little over the top for my taste, but hey, who was I to judge? Plus, I was here, wasn't I? I had come three hundred miles to meet one of the hundreds of cousins I had never met. That was something, wasn't it? At least I was trying to reconnect with a family tree whose branches had been lopped off by the tornado of feuding kin, scattered and broken by the age-old storm of Southern stubbornness. I could give myself credit for that, couldn't I?

Growing up I felt like an outsider among my friends, who flocked to their aunts' and uncles' homes to visit generations of cousins all bearing familial names and facial features reminiscent of Grandpa This and Such on one side or Grandma What's Her Name on the other. This child had Uncle Bubba's nose or Aunt Wilhemina's mouth. Another resembled Great-grandma Frieda's second cousin on her mother's side. Everyone was relieved that they hadn't inherited the monkey hair and blotchy skin of Uncle Scats. Southern families live and prosper by how many relatives we can accumulate, and by documenting who looks like whom. They keep track in family Bibles, which are passed down from generation to generation as a testament to who we are and who our children could look like if we're not careful to choose our husbands and wives wisely. But I had no family record to look back on. For a reason beyond my comprehension, my side of the Horst family had missed out.

Oh, I knew *about* my father's family, his siblings, Uncle Martin, Aunt Nona, Aunt Carla, Uncle Sonny and the flamboyant baby of the clan, Uncle Fritz. I also knew that each and every one of them had gone into the flower business in one way, shape or form, wholesale or retail, hocking stems on street corners out of an old ice cream truck or in a fine shop in the high-rent district of Birmingham. They also all owned the same nose, the Horst hook I call it. Yes, sadly, I have it, too. But that was the extent of my knowledge, other than the fact that they all lived in Irondale, Alabama, just south of Birmingham, on Horst Hill Road. All except my father, Otto, the oldest son, that is. He had moved us to Memphis long before I was even a twitch in his underdrawers.

"Can't take the competition," he told me once. "Families have enough to bicker about without adding business competition to the mix."

I was a kid. I didn't understand this logic. I wanted cousins. Everyone else had them, why didn't I?

Cousin Betty emerged from the kitchen, a home health care nurse at her side. The nurse had answered the door and ushered us into the sunroom. My sister-in-law, Joanna, had driven me over. She and my brother, John, had recently moved to Birmingham—one more Horst family to add to the string of Horsts that litter those Alabama hills—and had met Betty for the first time just a few months earlier when they accidentally discovered that Uncle Fritz had died. They showed up at Fritz' funeral to pay their respects and to the shock of the Birmingham kinfolk who had forgotten that our father, long-dead Uncle Otto, had kids. Needless to say, John and his wife were not met with hugs and kisses. Betty was the only cousin to acknowledge them. Now, she had become the long lost cousin John had never had, too.

I had unpacked my video camera and perched it on the side table under an arrangement of peach-colored roses, spiky fern fronds and dried purple status. I planned to document this little visit so my daughters could see with their own eyes that Horst relatives really do exist.

Betty moved slowly, but her eyes played touch football with everything in the room. Her cane danced about erratically in front of her like a swashbuckler's sword. I half expected her to jump back and holler, "En garde!"

Instead she said, "Hey there, y'all. Good Lord, how long has it been?"

I didn't want to say, "Since forever," so I just smiled and carefully hugged her neck. Had I ever met this woman, I wondered? Maybe a time or two, when I was a little kid. Betty's mother had been my Aunt Carla, a brazen woman who showered hot pink lipstick-coated kisses on young cheeks, had a real, live monkey living in her magnolia tree out back and a shed with a roof designed to look like the Flying Nun's winged hat. That is all I recalled about my aunt. That was enough, I figured. But now, as I sat in the sunroom with that aunt's daughter, I wondered if I should keep a look out for flying monkeys or swooping nuns.

"Sit, now, gone and sit," Betty said, gesturing downward. "No need to just stand there like you've risen for the Queen." She eased herself into the chair I had hoped she would choose for its best camera angle. Joanna and I lowered ourselves onto the couch. "I may move at a snail's pace," Betty said, "but I'm still kickin'. That chemo stuff can certainly do a number on a body, but it didn't kill me, so I'm feeling pretty spry that I managed to kick death in the butt—again." Her hands moved to adjust her straw crown. "How do you like my hat? Damn wigs itch my scalp. Can't wear um', but I've got hats, oh, Lordy, have I got some fine hats."

Joanna and I complimented it. I was a little slow on the uptake, though. I had assumed this woman would be sprawled out in the bed, gray and gasping for breath. Multiple Myeloma, they call it. Betty's six-months-to-live death sentence had miraculously been extended and was now creeping up on three years. Just looking at her, I was certain I knew why. This woman had spunk. I settled back into the couch

The Lederhosen Gang!

The Schusters

Fritz, Kathe, Friedl, Karin & Peter

cushions, feeling like I might just survive this meeting after all.

"So, you want to know about the family. Well, you've come to the right place. I've lived right here on Horst Hill my whole life. I know everything there is to know, plus a little."

I opened my mouth to comment and explain exactly why I had come, but before I had the chance to speak, she pointed a chubby finger at my camcorder.

"But with that damn contraption tracking my every word, I guess I'll have to watch my mouth and be sure I don't let any really big family faux pas slip out."

"No, please don't censor anything on my account," I interjected. "If you can, just let it rip. I write family stories for a living, not newspaper exposés. I'll try to be accurate. Plus, there's a good chance that the only people who'll read this will be my kids."

I asked a couple of benign questions to get her started, but she didn't need my direction. She jumped right in and let it roll.

"I was Pop's favorite, you know. He called me Betty Boop. My mother, your Aunt Carla, was his favorite daughter, so naturally I was the favorite grandchild. And since you weren't born yet, you didn't have a chance." She smiled at me and winked as if claiming a position she dared anyone to rebuff. "Law, he was a character. Wore dungaree overalls and a broad rimmed hat every livin' day of his life. He was shorter than you'd imagine, and plump. We'd call him a sweet-a-holic today. Didn't have hardly any teeth left in his head. And he was blind, you know, saw nothing but blackness. Oh, not from birth, you understand. He was in his twenties, I'd say, when the accident happened. His parents, our great grandparents—everyone called them Du Mie and Du Pie—were in the landscaping business. Pop lost his sight when dy-no-mite blew up in his face when he was clearing rocks."

She sat quietly for a minute. Her eyes wandered over to the window, past her patio to the old homeplace that used to sit just across her driveway. The view it held still remained, looking down on the greenhouses that once lay below it on a flat place cut into the hill.

"After Du Mie and Du Pie went to Glory, Pop inherited the hill. He had seven greenhouses, total, sprawled on that hill out yonder, where Uncle Fritz' wholesale house sits today. They were all made of flimsy glass. They used to whitewash the roof panes in the summer with a mixture of lye and water to keep the sun from getting too hot and ruining the plants. A storm came through one year and destroyed them all. Scattered shards of sparkling glass covered the hill like diamonds. It was so sad. But I do business with Regions Bank to this day, God love 'em. They were called The Exchange Bank back then, and their kindly Mr. Russell was the only banker who didn't think Pop was crazy. He lent him the money to rebuild, and I'll . . . I'll . . . I'll never forget him for that." Tears filled her eyes. She waved off the embarrassment with a rumpled green Kleenex, which fluttered in front of her face like a Luna moth. She paused for an instant until the lump in her throat dissipated, and she could go on.

"Pop grew not-just-a-little-bit of everything. Waves of sweet peas crawled up waterfalls of fishing line that fell from the ceiling, every kind of mum—daisy, pom pom, spider, football—snapdragons and larkspur. Oh, I can't name all the varieties; it would take me all day. But he knew every one. He knew when they were ready to be cut by the feel of their petals, the thickness of the stems and their scent. He popped the heads off mums everyday, plucked off the smaller buds so the larger ones could suck up more juice. He was something special to watch, he was. A blind man feeling his way through an ocean of the flowers he loved."

As a child, I had heard snippets of stories about my grandfather. I had even relayed one to my sister a few weeks before, only to be told that my imagination was working overtime. How do writers ever keep track of what's real, she had wondered? How can you keep the facts separate from what you make up and spin into stories, she had wanted to know? Had my memories gotten mixed up with my fiction? I wasn't sure, but I was here with Betty to find out.

"Long after your daddy, Uncle Otto, moved your family up north to Memphis," Betty said, "Pop got knocked in the head and robbed by one of the hired help, a Mr. Sammy Brown was his name. We took Pop to the University Hospital to get stitched up and, while we were there, a doctor by the name of Dr. Champ Lyons asked if he could take a look at Pop's eyes. Well, don't cha know, that Dr. Lyons told Pop he could help him see again. He had to pluck one eye out and replace it with glass, but the other one got fixed. Yep, Pop was the first person in the country, in the world, or at least in Alabama to lose his sight

and then have medical science give it back to him. His life story was even featured on that television show, *We The People*, from back in the fifties. They just loved to broadcast miracles. And, of course, me being the favorite, I got to fly on the airplane with him and my mother up to New York City to be on the show. That fancy TV producer man even came down here to get footage of the property. I have that old reel around here someplace. Now, where would I have stashed it? I sure was cute back then. I'll have to find it to let you see."

She glanced around the room as if it might be hidden under the leaves of the silk rhododendron or beside the urn of cascading plastic wisteria. The phone rang, her daughter, Heidi, checking in on her to make sure she was all right. When Betty resumed her story, a new sense of playfulness shined in her eyes.

"You know, Pop never let anything keep him from doing what he wanted to do. He had driven for years, even before his surgery and even though he was as blind as a possum in daylight. Back then, your daddy was the first to survive rides with Pop. As just a little tike, Uncle Otto would sit in Pop's lap and steer while Pop worked the pedals. Otto would yell, 'Slow down! Brake, brake, for God's sake Pop, BRAKE!'"

Betty's arms flew up and she stared wide-eyed into space as if she were riding along in the truck with Pop and my daddy, and scared to death they were about to run off the road. After a dramatic pause, she continued, "Of course it was all yelled in German. Pop spoke English as good or better than most, but here on Horst Hill, German was the language of choice. Lawhavemercy, they churned up gravel, mowed down mailboxes and scared the bejesus out of neighbors all over these hills. Pop wouldn't let the mild annoyance of being blind ruin his life."

It was clear to me that Betty had taken after her beloved Pop, probably more than she recognized. She had the spark of a drama queen who had stared cancer in the face and spit at it. I wondered if I had inherited that quality. Would I be so inclined to fight for my life if some horrible thing threatened to kick me in the knees, and do it with such fun-loving audaciousness? Or was that a Horst Hill family quality? Did only kinfolk who had lived on the hill, worked the greenhouses, or hocked flowers on the street corners of Birmingham have a chance to get in on that kind of family chutzpah?

"But Lord, after he got his eyesight back, he was worse than ever. He tossed me in the truck cab one Saturday morning. We usually rode the streetcar, but this day he was in rare form. We were headed to town to drop off a truckload of pigs at the market, to buy a box of broken cookies from the Dab's Cookie Factory and to sit at 'Wools-worth's' soda fountain. Oh, how he loved Coke floats! Anyway, we were clipping along down Old Leeds Road, and there ahead of us was a roadblock. The po-lice were checking driver's licenses. Now, Pop was certain they had set up right there at that spot 'cuz they knew he'd be coming down that hill and that he wouldn't want to get caught—again."

Betty leaned forward in her chair, bracing her elbows on her knees. She spoke right into my camera. So much for stage fright. She was working this amateur production with a dramatic dalliance that would make Scarlett O'Hara proud.

"Well, Pop came to a screeching halt right smack dab in the middle of Old Leeds. He wheeled that old truck around, pigs squealing, six— two hundred-and-fifty-pound pork chops shifting their weight in the back of the truck. Pop almost tossed us down the ravine, but somehow he managed to keep that old flatbed upright. We lost a few sideboards off the top railing, and the back panel wiggled loose, but managed to hang on. Next thing I know, sirens are blaring and we are in a high speed chase through the hills."

She stopped to catch her breath, but then she didn't continue. She relaxed back in her chair as if the story stopped right there and Joanna and I were supposed to accept the fact that we would never know how it ended. We tried to be patient, but Joanna couldn't take the suspense. "So, what happened next? Come on, Betty, you can't bring us to the edge like that and then drop us. Did y'all get away?"

Betty smiled like the devil. "Hell no! O'course we got caught. What'd ya' think? The po-lice pulled us over and had that ticket written before they even got up beside the truck. Pop bounded out of the cab, madder than all those pigs that were just coming back to their senses and wanting out bad. Pop cussed that officer up one hill and down the other, all in German of course so he couldn't write down any of his curse words and make them a part of the report."

She fished around for the handle of her cane. I thought she wanted to get up, so I rose to offer a hand, but she waved me off. "Just readjusting," she explained. She wiggled her hips back into her chair. I sat back down and she picked up where she'd left off.

"Well, I thought for sure they were going to haul us both in. I must have been about twelve years old, at the most. I've never been so thrilled and terrified in my whole life. Pop wadded up the ticket and tossed it into the truck bed with the pigs. The po-lice took the keys from the ignition, leaving us to walk home—or so they thought. Well, they hadn't cleared the bend in the road before Pop had that sucker hot-wired and here we went again. A little thing like breaking the law wasn't going to stop Pop from his Coke float or getting his pigs to town."

Betty paused again and motioned to the corner of the room for the nurse to hand her something to drink. The woman pretended not to notice the gestures. She just lifted her *Woman's Day* a little higher and turned the page. Joanna got up and retrieved a glass of water from the kitchen. Betty looked a little disappointed with Joanna's choice of refreshment, but she drank it down with only the slightest hint of a sour face.

"Pop wanted nothing more in the world than to have his very own driver's license. Everyone thought he was crazy. We all knew that, with his police record, and the fact that one of his eyes saw perfectly, but the other one was cold dead glass, no Department of Motor Vehicles employee would be stupid enough to grant our Pop a license of his own. Well, Pop got a mad-on one morning. He snatched me up and made Uncle Fritz drive us into town. He said, "As soon as I get myself a license, I'm going to the au-to-mo-bile showroom and buy myself a new truck." He had dressed for the occasion, too. He wore his Sunday-go-to-meeting suit, shined shoes and a bow tie. He looked like he was ready to take on the Governor if they denied him his fondest wish in the whole wide world.

"Uncle Fritz pulled up in front of the courthouse, across from the First Christian Church. We had to park there and walk to the DOT office for Pop to take the test. Well, don't you know, he sailed right through it, answered every one of those questions without so much as a glass-eyed blink. He was so excited I thought Fritz was going to have to tie him to a post."

Betty's emotions failed her again. Her green Kleenex took flight, and a long sigh escaped her. She took her time collecting herself. Joanna and I leaned forward to hear the rest.

"In those days, you took your test at the DOT office, and then you had to go to the courthouse to pick up your license and get your picture made. Well, Pop danced all the way. He kicked his heels like a Russian squat dancer, swinging around parking meters and tipping his hat to every livin' person who passed our way. Fritz was a little embarrassed, but I danced right along with him. I was so happy that he would finally be able to drive without having to worry about getting caught for doing what he loved."

Betty lifted her straw hat and rubbed her baldness with a trembling hand. Her painted on eyebrows raised and lowered with her heavy breaths. "When we came up on our truck parked at the base of the courthouse steps, Pop noticed that our meter was just about out of

time. Well, now that he was a law-abiding citizen about to get his official driver's license, he couldn't let the meter run down and take the chance of being a criminal all over again. So, he stopped to drop a nickel in the meter, and his heart just up and quit."

Betty hands fell into her lap and her head bowed with all the finality of a last curtain call. She stared at her splotchy appendages like they belonged to Pop himself. She shook her head.

Joanna and I just sat there, unable to speak. We wanted this to be another of Betty's dramatic tactics to keep us enthralled. We were sure she would spring back to life, all smiles, and go on with the story, explaining that Pop was fine, he just had indigestion from all of his excitement and jumping about. Or that he was just funning with them and trying to scare them into thinking he was sick.

Finally, she looked up and said, "Pop died right there on the spot, slumped over the parking meter. He never got his driver's license and never got to drive legally by himself. Of course, he never got his new truck, either. Uncle Fritz was real upset about that."

Now it was my turn to tear up. Joanna followed suit. We bawled like children slapped for no good reason. How could this be? Family stories are supposed to end happy. And remarkably, Betty didn't seem to be upset. She sat quietly and watched her two newly discovered relatives struggle to come to grips with the death of a grandfather we had met, fallen in love with and lost, all within the hour and through the vivid pictures painted by this beloved granddaughter.

I had never met my grandfather, but I now felt that I knew him. I had grown to love him in only minutes and claimed him as my own. I felt proud to have had him, to have his blood coursing through my veins and to have passed it on to my girls. But I now mourned his loss. I wished my father had told me more. I wished I had known more about these Alabama relatives, no matter the family disagreements or competitiveness, no matter the inherent craziness that litters my gene pool and makes normal seem impossible to attain. This is who we are. Why not embrace it? We could not be considered Southern without a small multitude of colorful and unstable relations scattered about in our storm-battered family tree.

Joanna and I composed ourselves, and Betty went on to relate many more Horst stories that September afternoon. Like real life, few had happy endings.

But after we'd recovered from them, we piled into Betty's fire engine red Caddy and tossed some of our own Horst Hill gravel to the wind.

"I may not be able to walk worth a flip," she hollered over her shoulder as she spun out of her driveway headed up the hill, "but I can drive. Hold on to my hat, lovebug. I'd hate to lose this one. It's one of my favorites. Pop may not have gotten his license, but those fools down at the DOT gave me mine. And it is my mission in life to let Pop live vicariously through my automotive high jinx. Let's roll!"

Later that evening, as I stood at the bathroom sink at my brother's house removing my makeup, my reflection caught my attention like it hadn't done since I was a child. I turned to survey my profile. Maybe my Horst hook wasn't so bad after all. I had never really considered a nose job, but it felt good to finally be satisfied.

It's funny how families change over the years. My ideas about those crazy Birmingham relatives that my father had to get away from for the sake of his sanity and the safety of his kids now seemed like a child's imagination run wild. It was only distance that had kept us apart, not some horrid mutation in the gene pool. I'm sure my daddy had his reasons for us not visiting Birmingham more often, but suddenly uncovering the mystery didn't matter anymore. I no longer felt cheated out of relatives. Some are still there on Horst Hill, or thereabouts, and others are scattered across the country. But I hope some are researching our family history on the Internet and with those computerized genealogy CD's, and wondering which long lost grand-someone their kids look like.

I know I am.

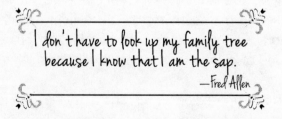

I don't have to look up my family tree because I know that I am the sap.
— Fred Allen

# The Dance

A pimple-pink rose bloomed on the
tip of her sun-kissed nose,
the magenta bump threatening a good fester,
but only delivering high color and a blush
of embarrassment whenever Thomas or
a secret crush happened by.
Soap and water, love, daily and gently,
rinse three times, pat dry.
The pimple-pink rose, determined to
stay just long enough to visit her first dance.

Except for the point,
the still point,
there would be no dance,
and there is only the dance.
—Thomas Stearns Eliot

# The Linebacker Poet

I had just finished reading a stack of "mandatory" submissions to the annual 7th grade *Footprints of the Junior High Soul* publication when Michael Thompson, acclaimed expert on the development of boys and author of the bestselling book *Raising Cane*, called our faculty meeting to order. I placed my red pen aside and readied myself to take notes as Mr. Thompson began to speak. He had been invited by my school to address topics related to the unique teaching opportunities that boys present teachers and parents. His appearance had been preceded by much publicity and our faculty felt privileged to have him all to ourselves before his scheduled public appearance later that evening. The conference room buzzed with anticipation as teachers, deans and school board members filed in and took their seats. Being a new junior high teacher, I was especially eager to listen to this renowned authority speak, hoping, quite frankly, that he would solve my classroom management woes and give me useful pointers about how to instill a love of learning in my male students, as everything I had tried lately had failed miserably.

Thompson's presentation focused on the challenges adolescent boys pose in the traditional classroom setting. He discussed several reasons for these challenges, not the least of which was the number of erections adolescent boys experience and must ignore in the course of a day. I was engrossed by his presentation as I gained new insight into the behavior of boys. I nodded at appropriate comments to my colleagues while praying silently that some intelligent thought would materialize in my mind so that I, too, might contribute effectively to the discussion and prove once and for all to myself and others present that choosing to teach junior high had been the correct career choice for me.

I watched the minutes tick by, however, and was dismayed by my lack of contributory effort. If I didn't come up with something to offer soon, my incompetence would surely become obvious. Try as I might, nothing came to me. My mind was a vacuum. I tucked my chin and hoped no eyes would fall upon me.

Then it happened. Mr. Thompson mentioned something about his desire to find one example that would encapsulate the thinking processes of an adolescent boy. Ah ha, I thought. Here's my chance. I had a whole stack of a junior high ramblings in the submissions I had been plodding through before the meeting began. Now, if I could just find one to share. I shuffled through my papers with one hand, hoping my eager fingers would fall upon just the right one to fulfill Mr. Thompson's dream. I waved my other hand like the smartest kid in class to the tune of, "Oooo, oooo, call on me, call on me!"

> *No one can make you feel inferior without your consent*
> —Anna Eleanor Roosevelt

Finally, Mr. Thompson nodded my way. I beamed at the acknowledgement, stood ceremoniously, and read a poem titled "Big Mac," written by my student, Brock Gaines.

> *I wonder what I will eat tonight*
> *I wonder what I will wear tomorrow*
> *I wonder what I will do tomorrow*
> *I wonder who is gay or straight.*
> *I wonder who lives in the projects*
> *I wonder if I am the real Brock Gaines.*
> *I wonder how they make the Big Mac*
> *I wonder what they use in the Special Sauce*

Midway through my recitation of Brock's poem an image of myself standing in the unemployment line flashed before me. Why did I read this poem, I wondered. Of all the wonderful examples of creative writing in my stack, how could I have chosen this one, I asked myself. You see, Brock Gaines was a linebacker on the junior high football team. He hated to write. He reacted regularly and gutturally to my writing assignments and pronouncements that "all we must do to be writers is to think of ourselves as writers." Brock's journal entries were usually curt and defensive. They reflected a boredom born of raging hormones longing to express themselves in more physical ways. And now, I had chosen Brock's poem to read aloud to an expert on boys!

Mr. Thompson extended his hand and, shaking now, I handed over Brock's scrawled poetic offering. Silence draped the room as Michael Thompson's powerful baritone reread "Big Mac" aloud. I watched in shocked pause as my colleagues absorbed the words and took them to heart, and I realized in that instance that I had missed it. I had read Brock's words without giving them the respect they deserved. Hearing them again now, read with honor and an open mind, I finally recognized the profound wisdom they contained.

"This is the perfect snapshot of the mind of a junior high boy," Mr. Thompson announced. "I can lecture all day, but no one can sum up the unique workings of a boy better than a boy himself."

Michael Thompson pulled me aside after his lecture and asked me to please contact Brock and his parents to see if they would grant him permission to use "Big Mac" in his lecture that night and in future speaking engagements he had planned. I'll never forget the look on Brock's face when I told him.

"My poem, Mrs. Schuster?" he said. "You can't mean my poem."

"Yes, Brock, your poem. Sometimes we don't recognize our talents until someone else points them out to us."

I was recently reminded of this opportunity for learning as I read Frank Smith's *The Book of Learning and Forgetting*. Mr. Smith explains the classic view of learning as being, ". . . not hard work. Something is being learned, whether we want it or not, all the time. But achieving the necessary circumstances and frame of mind for desired learning may be very difficult indeed."

Yes, difficult. I now strive to be more open to those necessary circumstances. I read my students' work with different eyes. I no longer look for proper punctuation or grammar, at least not on the first go-round. I no longer allow my own prejudices to mar their freshness.

Neither do I inspect them with a stereotypical lens of the author intact. I have altered my frame of mind. Instead, I reverence each offering and try to glean the extraordinary from it because in order for me to recognize my own talents as a writer and a teacher I must first recognize that I am a student with much to learn.

# *Going Home*

We parked on the street, right out front, and approached the half-clapboard, half-brick façade like a young couple inspecting the prospect of settling down. Young at heart, anyway. The house stood empty, pitiful in its shabbiness, the sad face of the *For Sale* sign listing decidedly to the left and leaning facedown toward the ground. A few days ago I had watched the present owner weed the front beds and cut the knee-high grass. He did this with all the property owner pride of a slumlord, pearls of sweat dribbling down his neck as he slugged along. I'd happened by on my way to the midtown library and had used cut-through streets, those indelibly etched in the personal mapping system that growing up in a place lends a young mind. I hadn't known the house was for sale before that day, and had not been able to get the old place off my mind since. Now, standing on the walkway leading to the front door, a giddiness born of something foreign and childlike welled up in me and its eagerness to get inside took control.

I'd brought him here because I wanted him to know me, not just in the ways we had already grown close, but really know me, in the visceral ways potential life partners enjoy. He needed to understand where I came from and what forces of nature and nurture had clashed in my puberty and young teen years to cause the emotional minefield I had turned out to be. I'd prepare him, I figured. It was only fair. That way, if he tucked tail and ran south, I'd be able to say, "Good riddance," without feeling wounded, and with the recognition that he couldn't handle the complications my parents had dished out on me. I admit he'd racked up some major points when he'd agreed to come along. Just curious, I figured. Better yet, just crazy. But accompanying me on this little adventure into my past and surviving it were two different things.

After a few restless minutes of groping through windows, we moved around the side of the house. He didn't object when I jimmied the side door of the garage using a ballpoint pen like I used to do when I'd stayed out past curfew and didn't want to give myself away. He just jingled the change in his jeans pockets, glancing from side to side as if a cop might round the corner, as if someone cared that two paunched and graying 1970s pot-heads had returned to their failed life of crime. The latch clicked and released. I smiled, the familiar rush of misbehavior filling me again.

Pushing against the door with my shoulder, it gave way in a gush of dust motes and slashed light. I fanned the air, and the milky figures of my father and brothers greeted me like ancient ghosts released from an Egyptian auto parts tomb as if they had always been there, and had never crawled out from under their latest dune buggy project or rebuilt Mustang. The scent of stale motor oil and welder's salt embraced me like the chilled hands of a stalker. Childhood had been the pits. Shaking—with either some kind of masochistic excitement or anticipated dread, I couldn't be sure which—I crossed the blackened floor. Twenty-five years and nothing had changed.

> When I speak of home, I speak of a place where — in default of a better — those I love are gathered together; and if that place were a gypsy's tent, or a barn, I should call it by the same good name notwithstanding.
>
> —Charles Dickens, from *Nickolas Nickelby*

When I turned, I found that he had followed. His eyes wandered like mine around the musty space, then they met, my hazel to his brown. Only for a moment . . . I blinked.

More points. He was doing okay so far, I thought.

Granulated floor cleaner crunched beneath our Birkenstocks as we passed the garage's heart, where years of oil leaks had joined forces to leave their mark. The scent it kicked up reminded me of elementary school when the janitor was called out to clean up vomit in the hallway.

But as we neared the kitchen door, I noticed the stationary vice grip still bolted to the workbench Daddy had built when I was six. In one swipe, all masculine and elementary school scents were dispelled. Vomit and welder's salt were replaced with the comforting fragrances of fresh coconut, seven-minute icing and white cake as light as air. I hadn't expected any good memories. Where had these come from? Could my determination to forever wallow in my teenage misfortunes really wimp out on me now? Fail me after so many years of practice?

I placed my hand on the vice crank like mother had taught me. The black eyes of a coconut looked up at me now. "Gently—turn it slowly, child," Mother had said, the bulk of her leaning forward, the tail of her floral apron protecting her hand from the bristled coconut orb and keeping it from popping out as the vice squeezed. I could still feel her there, with chisel poised on the spot, just to the left of those shadowy coconut eyes, her hammer raised like a tomahawk eager for blood. She whacked once, twice, never three times, and a fine fissure erupted across the scalp of the nut, just wide enough to allow us entrance into its delicate center without losing the milky nectar that hid within its womb. I closed my eyes to hold onto this vision, to keep it from fading back into the recesses from which it came. But it vanished, sucked back by the vacuum of remembrance to a cavern where ancient relics hide until they are called into duty to compress against one's chest and draw choking lumps to the back of one's throat. Not even the creamy sweetness of imagined icing left its essence on my tongue.

His hand touched my arm. A surprise so tender, so understanding. Another point, I figured, or maybe even two.

The kitchen door was unlocked. Why bother, we'd always reasoned, since the garage doors protected the outer perimeter of the house? Guess the present owners shared the same philosophy. It swung open easily, but with the creak of arthritic hinges now. "WD-40 will fix that up," Daddy's voice whispered in my ear from the grave. A shiver of longing quaked across the landscape of my skin. Oh, to hear him say that in person again. Had he been as gruff as I remembered? Or had his bark come from caring? His criticism from a love he didn't have a clue how to share?

Lowe's weekly special white-on-white linoleum now covered and failed to conceal the uneven ridges of Mother's faux brick beneath. The gaping refrigerator hole stood empty, filthy, like an open wound with a copper artery coiling out for a spigot to bring it back to life. The cabinets had been painted off white, the best for resale—What color had they not been?—but the poorly glued edges of cheap Formica curled up along the perimeter of the countertop revealing the negligence of renovators who owned no stake in the place.

My eyes scanned the space, half expecting Mother to barge in with bagged groceries, or John to yell from the den for me to bring him a root beer. My eyes paused of their own accord at a spot over the sink. The metal hook remained where Tweetie's cage had hung in the front window until the water disaster of 1965 when a pipe had burst. A fountain had erupted from Mother's new dishwasher and spewed steaming clear lava all the way up to the ceiling, a scalding storm that quickly flooded the kitchen and made the cabinets seem like the gushing banks of Niagara Falls. Tweetie's panicked squawks still rang in my ears, as shrill and desperate as a woman being raped. I had rushed in without thinking, bare feet and all. A kitchen chair boosted me onto the countertop river, but I lost my footing on the way down and crashed hard to the floor. The *crack* of my femur still punctuates my nightmares, as the ripping of flesh still sets my teeth on edge. I glanced down and found my finger tracing the ragged scar where the cage had slashed me. It runs from below my elbow to my shoulder, and has become to me a comfort, stroked unconsciously, rhythmically like the soothing edge of a baby blanket to a toddler, a lasting reminder that I almost lost my life trying to save that bird.

"These floors are in great shape."

My husband's voice wrenched me back to the present, echoed from the dining room where gleaming hardwoods bounced his baritone around like rocks in a can. He had already moved on with no visions, no memories to tangle him up. I wished for the capacity, the ability to move forward without the need to look back. But examining the past holds freedom, doesn't it? Isn't that why I'd come? To exorcize the phantoms that tortured my dreams?

The living room seemed barren with the pale wood exposed. Still, I slipped out of my shoes without thinking. My right foot pushed them aside to toe the wall, both soles resting on the kitchen side of the boundary to the dining room. The walls now shone in a pale caramelized eggshell, a much more pleasing tone than the turquoise of my youth. Dust mote fairies drifted through the air, riding on a cloud scented with old talc, fresh polyurethane and rat bait.

I remembered the day Sissie had graduated from Interior Design school. She had convinced Mother to be her first guinea pig and let her redecorate in the newest shades—harvest gold, avocado green and that putrid shade of turquoise thrown in. They worked for months on the living room transformation, Daddy griping daily about the cost of creating what he called "the mausoleum effect." But Mother deserved fashionable decency, Sissie said. If Daddy wouldn't buy Mother a respectable house on Sequoia three streets over, Sissie was determined to give this Cracker Jack box the polish only her expertise could allow. But when she finished, even I realized that she'd taken "trend" to an unhealthy level. The carpet chosen had been a looped pile, gold and turquoise weaving a pattern so dramatic that it undulated underfoot and made me feel as if the ocean had moved in with us and its purpose was to keep me off balance and nauseous in my own home. The floral fabric of the couch had only added to the upset; its greenness mimicked nausea so well. Metallic gold chairs had flanked the picture window, which Sissie had draped in yards and yards of fabric so heavy it sagged into deep folds off the curtain rods. It shaded the once airy window like thick sunglasses against a blaring sun.

He must have sensed my distraction, but how did he know, I wondered. I was pretending so well, wasn't I? He was on the verge of pity, I was sure. Yes, a sad flicker at the back of his pupils alerted me to the change. His feelings had already soured, now that he'd seen the shabby digs of my youth. It was inevitable, of course. I realized that now. What was I thinking bringing him here? He took my hand and led me away.

We moved down the tight hallway toward my bedroom. Just a few more feet. My sanctuary by day, the tiny room at the end of the hall was where my creativity had bloomed in spite of the turmoil outside its door. A hormonal mother, a distant father and two brothers, whose missions in life were to make my life miserable. I'd been tortured by them, hadn't I? I had realized this questionable fact on my eighteenth birthday, the day I married the first of my mistakes. I had held onto that myth ever since. Now, standing on the cusp of yet another marital mishap, I wondered if any of it really mattered. What if I just chose to forget? What if I shrugged it off and said, "To hell with it all?" Could a person do that? Forget where they came from? Forgive whatever wrongs bound them? Place it all in a specimen jar marked, "Dead Baggage," and leave it on a closet shelf and walk away? I doubted this.

My spirit lifted as we moved toward my bedroom. If I could just make it there, if he could see the place I never rested he would grasp the essence of my imaginary self, instead of the *who* I no longer wanted to be. Our steps seemed in slow motion, excruciating in their deliberateness. The room seemed so far, far away.

Then it happened.

The bathroom grabbed me upon passing. Its withered hand gripped my sleeve and dragged me from my mission of peace. Sanctuary would have to wait. I turned right at its doorway and entered without putting up a fight. At the bathroom's heart, just as my reflection met me in the medicine cabinet mirror, I turned back to face him and closed the door before he had the chance to follow me inside.

I'm sure he thought I had to pee. He didn't knock or call out or jiggle the doorknob. Another point or two in his favor. If he'd touched the door, I would have surely succumbed to the memory that now threatened to drown me, the memory of that morning, the memory of shattered innocence, red water and stained bubbles that left a pink tinge of shame in the bottom of our lily-white tub.

The morning had been crisp and a bit cool for the second week of May, just one week before my high school graduation in 1974. Mother had shaken me awake to let me know that Sissie was picking her up to take her to Midtown. Catherine's Stout Shoppe was having a sale. They wouldn't be gone long, she'd said. They planned to beat the crowds and be there when the store opened. Mother had trouble finding clothes that flattered her robust figure and depended on Sissie's fashion sense to steer her away from what Sissie called the "tented, muumuu look." I rolled over, dozing and compliant, happy for the extra shut-eye and looking forward to many more similar mornings as a high school grad. I don't know what time it was when the doorbell rang.

At first I tried to ignore it, but Mother had made Daddy install the Cadillac of all doorbell chimes a few years before, the kind that repeated the full eight-tone gong of enthusiastic church bells each time the button was compressed. We all hated the thing. Neighborhood children would push the button incessantly, just to make Mother mad, and then run away, laughing. Daddy had threatened often to rip the thing out of the wall, but Mother loved her chimes.

I was surprised and relieved that a friendly face greeted me when I'd opened the door.

"Hey. Hi! Oh, gee, what are you doing here?" I asked, my hand already fishing through the potpourri dish next to the entry for the key to the wrought iron and glass security door. I inserted the key into the deadbolt. The last sane thing I remember hearing was the chu-chunk of the tumblers' song.

I'd only been dating him a week, if you can call hanging out in a group of other teens dating, but what a week it had been. My first real boyfriend. I'd met him at the mall. He knew someone's brother, or was someone's cousin, had played football for Overton, was graduating next week, too, was going to UT on

> *An optimist is a guy that has never had much experience.*
> —Donald Robert Marquis, from "certain maxims of archy"

scholarship, was perfect, popular, muscular, handsome, like no one I'd ever dreamed would ever speak to me, notice me, be interested in me, me, me, a homely Thespian and art major . . . me. His eyelashes were longer and darker than any I'd ever seen.

Standing on the porch, he wore the smile and twinkle of adoration, eager and promising. I readjusted my ponytail, needing something to do with my hands, and twisted it into a quick bun to conceal its dishevelment from just rolling out of bed. I smoothed the front of my baggy T-shirt, then thought better of the action and pulled it away from my braless chest. I wished I'd gotten up when Mother woke me, wished I'd taken a shower, gotten dressed, had been ready for his visit, ready to welcome him into my home for the first time. He was happy to see me, he said. Happy I was home. He was just driving by and in the neighborhood. Thought he'd take the chance and stop by. "How long will your mother and sister be gone?"

His question didn't register until much later. I was too nervous, too giddy. I'd never entertained a boy before. I ushered him to the den, struggling to disguise my nerves and my excitement, but also wondering how Mother would react, if she knew I'd let someone into the house when she wasn't home. We had rules about such things, rules I had never considered breaking, rules I had never dreamed I'd have the opportunity or desire to break.

A week's worth of newspapers were stacked on the floor next to Daddy's recliner. His ashtray overflowed with butts and ash. The afghan Mother would never finish crocheting lay strewn across the couch. Its orange and harvest gold wool umbilicus twisted into a mass as it trailed to the floor toward the balls of yarn that gave it birth. I wondered what time it was, but had no point of reference. Mid-morning, certainly, I figured. I wondered if my brother, John, would come home for lunch on this first day of his summer job painting swimming pools. I wondered if Mother was in a dressing room, struggling with a zipper, if Sissie was helping her, or if they would barge in at any minute and ruin my very first moment alone with a beau.

His hand was dry and hot. It encircled mine, softly at first, then with great pressure. The fingers of his other hand tilted my chin up to meet his eyes. Those eyes. But his lashes now cast a shadow over the adoration I'd witnessed at the front door.

"You are my girl," he was saying, "no one else's. You adore me, and me only. You will never look at anyone else. Do you understand?"

Yes, yes, but no, I didn't. Why was he squeezing my hand so tightly? Was he angry? But why? What had I done? What was wrong? I wanted to ask him. What do you mean? No, I didn't flirt with anyone else last night.

I looked up, but only as far as the faucet. I'd been staring at the sink drain. I needed to look into the mirror. If I could manage that one feat, I might survive this twenty-five-year-old nightmare. Seeing myself could bring me back to the present, where aged crow's feet and frown lines could jolt me with a good shot of reality. But the mirror held its own memories. I wasn't sure I could do it, go there, handle any more.

A new white frame had been added by the homeowner to dress up the mirror. I avoided my reflection, instead focusing on the frame as my fingers tugged. The medicine cabinet swung open. Its scratched and rusted metal interior had not been replaced. Thin glass shelves stood empty. Rings of rust lined the bottom shelf where moist shaving cream cans had left their brand. I remembered sitting on the toilet seat as a child and watching Daddy lather his cheeks with thick white foam. He'd rake one side of his double-edged blade across his stubble, shake it off in the sink water, then spin it around and go to work on his chin with the other side. He never used a blade more than twice. Too dull for his whiskers, he'd said. "Got to have a sharp one every other day." He'd twist the razor open and gently lift the dulled blade between his finger and thumb. A tiny slit in the back wall of the medicine cabinet was "the safest place to dispose of them," he'd told me, dropping the blade into the dark abyss behind the wallboard and between the 2x4 studs that stood "sixteen inches of center" in the wall. "Don't want to put something sharp as this in the trashcan," Daddy had warned me. "Could cut a finger off, or worse, if you weren't careful, and that would hurt like all hell," he'd said.

I remember thinking, *what a great hiding place. No one could ever find you down there.* But that was before *it* happened, before that day when Mother's door chimes and the deadbolt's song had changed my life. I wrote my first note that day. Sitting on the toilet seat, hands shaking, I jotted my pain onto the paper wrapper of a toilet paper roll. I folded it neatly, creasing and smoothing the offering, and pushed it gently into the best hiding place I could think of. I visualized the razors shredding it into nonexistence, slicing it into pieces so small it could no longer be read, no longer be real.

Now, the tiny slit in the back of the medicine cabinet expanded under my focus. It widened, black and menacing, like a toothless mouth reaching out to swallow me up. Deep, deep. I succumbed to the bite and fell to the digestive bottom of the wall's belly, knowing Daddy's razors would greet me and slice me into ribbons of aching flesh. I welcomed the slashing. I remembered wondering as a child how many years it would take to fill up that space. How many razorblades, stacked sliver upon sliver, would it take to fill and overflow the space? More than he could ever use, I remember figuring. So I'd added to the collection. Once, twice, many, many times. I wrote notes and offered them to the depths. Note after note. Addressed to no one. Delivered to the darkness. Both confession and comfort. Confessor and Comforter. Pain fluttering down toward the wish of destructive healing that would never come.

The need to measure the stack consumed me now. If I could only count the destruction, rank its height, width and breadth, maybe I could rationalize its ravages and somehow visualize a more minimal effect it had had on my life. I gripped the mirror's frame and pulled, applying more muscle to the hinged side to compensate for the side that wasn't attached. It gave way much easier than I'd expected, tilting toward me and slipping from my grasp. I let it fall. Shards of mirror rained down onto the tile floor. Splinters of reflection littered the area around my bare feet. Tiny droplets of blood welled up from each strike.

> No coward soul is mine,
> No trembler in the world's storm-
>     troubled sphere:
> I see Heaven's glories shine,
> and faith shines equal,
> arming me from fear.
> —Emily Bronte, from Last Lines

I didn't hear the pounding on the door, or his screams through it. I shoved the mangled medicine cabinet aside and, in one fluid motion, mounted the sink, my jeaned knees balancing on the porcelain lip. Peering down into the gaping hole, my eyes parted the black void as if healing beams directed them on this cause. The bathroom door crashing inward created suction. The wall seemed to bellow a great burp, dusty air blowing up from its depths into my eyes, the wind of it tossing my hair from my face. Pain escaped me through its gushing, and with it the remains of my misery, either sliced into molecular particles as I'd imagined or decomposed from so many years of being buried in the dark.

His hands were moist upon my arms, their pressure light and reassuring. He guided me gently from the bathroom, down the hall, through the kitchen and into the garage. He didn't ask; I didn't tell him. The door we'd jimmied closed behind us and I relinquished the need to visit this place again.

# Mary Horst's Fresh Coconut Cake

1 cup butter
2 cups sugar
5 eggs
1 teaspoon baking soda
dash salt
2¾ cups cake flour
1 teaspoon baking powder
¾ cup buttermilk
½ cup fresh coconut milk
1 teaspoon vanilla
½–¾ teaspoon coconut flavoring
2 recipes Never Fail 7-Minute Icing
2 cups fresh grated coconut

Cream butter and sugar until light and fluffy. Add eggs, one at a time. Combine dry ingredients in separate bowl. Add vanilla to buttermilk. Alternate adding wet and dry ingredients, ending with dry. Add coconut flavoring last, mixing to incorporate.

Pour batter into 2 (9 inch) greased and floured cake pans. Bake 350 degrees for 35-40 minutes.

Ice with Mary Horst's Never-Fail 7-Minute Icing. (recipe on next page)

# Mary Horst's Never-Fail 7-Minute Icing

1 cup sugar
1/4 teaspoon salt
1/2 teaspoon cream of tarter
2 unbeaten egg whites
3 tablespoons water
1 teaspoon vanilla

Combine all ingredients, except vanilla, in the top of a double boiler. Use hand-mixer to stir. Beat briskly for 3 minutes or until frosting is fluffy and makes stiff peaks. Remove from stove and add vanilla.

Makes enough for 2—9 inch layers, but Mother always made 2 recipes because I couldn't keep my fingers out of the bowl.

Notice please that my mother left out the most important (secret) ingredient: fresh coconut milk.

I can still see her wink at me whenever I saw her slip it into the batter, as if only I was privy to her secret. Everyone knew, of course, but we respected her enough to never say, "Don't forget the coconut milk!" aloud.

Here's winking at you!

# *Silence*

Hearing a great silence,
I asked the Spirit to speak through me
—with wisdom about life . . . and love.

I am unsure about this great silence with which you tease me, this silence of surrender and enlightenment. I want to find it, to discover its secrets and the form to use to attain it, as if in its capture it might transform into a floppy-eared bunny whose fur and snuggle could calm me and make me whole. I trust that you have a plan for introducing this silence to my life. Writing may be the gateway . . . or not. You've never heard the noise I create on paper. It might shatter the fluffy silence that you say will heal me and bring me peace. But . . . but . . . but is a big word. I believe you can do it. I know I cannot achieve it alone. So, to you I plead: Grant me silence. Show me peace.

In the beginning was the Word,
And the Word stretched into sentences,
And we dwelt among them.

In that dwelling I got swallowed up. The dialogue of shame and pain shortened the fading beauty of my lyrical ode, chopped it, stanza by stanza, into rumblings and bellows—no rhyme scheme, no meter, just static and premature blasts.

On the day of our birth, we
Were sentenced to life—
A life sentence, earned and learned
word by word.

Just when I think I've earned something, anything, there is more earning to be done, more struggle. But now, at my elder age, I face each in a little better way. Oh, I still ponder too much (another word for worry). I still fail to maintain a grasp on that illusive self-confidence. For the most part, however, I turn to you more often and sooner than in earlier days. For this I am grateful. This whisper of quiet . . . I still know little of the silence I long to know well.

The soul is wisdom's echo chamber—
where words resound.

So it is the words that live in me, not crazy characters that shake me awake and force me to take their dictation? Reassurance personified.

A word on the page is
The heaviest object in the universe.
It cannot be lifted.

# *Dandelions & Crabgrass*

Have you ever been scared? I mean really, really scared? Shake your shoes right off your feet scared? Well, I have. And I have to tell you; it ain't all it's cracked up to be. No, siree, I don't like it one little bit, especially because my particular scare has to do with someone real, someone I know. I'm not talking about being scared of the dark—at almost eight years old, I'm way past that—or even scared like you get when you've watched one too many episodes of *The Twilight Zone*. Yes, *episode* is a big word because I'm a big girl and I like using words none of my friends know. I'm talking the kind of scared that makes the hairs on your arms stand at attention long after the scariness has passed by. My bestest friend in the whole wide world is Angela Marie Chandler Thompkins. I'm not sure why, but everyone calls her Marie Chandler and drops her first name completely off, like it's not even there. I'm also not sure why she has so many names, but Mother says it's because Mrs. Thompkins is from Georgia and Georgia women think they all have *Tara* in their blood and that hoop skirts are coming back in style. I'm not sure what all that means either, but I am sure that I don't think Mother likes Mrs. Thompkins very much. Maybe Mother wishes she were from Georgia, too. Or maybe she thinks having Tara in your blood is better than having Mississippi or Smith in it, like we've got. We live in Mississippi and Smith is our last name. But Mother's last name used to be Gaston, before she married Daddy and changed it to suit his "fragile ego." I think maybe Gaston made her feel more like Tara makes Mrs. Thompkins feel. Smith must have taken all of Mother's Tara right out of her. The hoop skirts are a whole other thing, I believe. Anyway, Marie Chandler lives one house down from me. Some old lady lives between us. We call her Mrs. Bridgefort to her face, real polite-like, because that's her name, but my mind comes up with lots of other names for her when I'm sneaking across her front yard to get to Marie Chandler's house. *Mrs. Bugger-nose. Mrs. Busy-bottom.* She doesn't like us to set foot in her yard. I don't understand this reasoning. What else is grass for, if it ain't to be walked on, I want to know. *Mrs. Bossy-britches.* Marie Chandler is not very good at sneaking. She gets caught every time. *Mrs. Brigger-doodle* yells out her kitchen window, "Scat, you little Dickens. Sidewalks were made for children, not my beautiful lawn." Daddy says her "beautiful lawn" is more like an animal garden with its chief sources of vegetation being her bumper crop of dande*lions* and *crab*grass. Mother always shushes him, saying, "She's an old woman, Hube. Leave her alone." Marie Chandler doesn't like *Mrs. Bridge-of-doom*, either, but she is not as tough as I am. Whenever Marie Chandler gets caught crossing *Mrs. Buggerfort's* yard, she always bursts into tears, throws her hands into the air, and runs, bawling and squalling, back home as if the old hag had told her she was ugly as a stump, or that she was too dumb to ever get married and have kids. I'll never understand why Marie Chandler turns and runs back to her house, when she's good as halfway to my house whenever she gets caught. Seems like to me that she'd just pick up her pace and blast on past the woman. But no, she leaves the rescuing up to me. I don't mess around about it either. **Simper Fi**, as Daddy always says. Never abandon a comrade in need. I strut right on out there, my right leg lifted high in the air for the first step onto the forbidden property. "Hey, hey there," I yell out toward the house, bounding forward, goose-stepping like a Russian soldier marching to impress her general. "Mrs. Bridgefort, ma'am. Yes, it's me, coming through. It's Amy Smith crossing your yard this time. But only for a minute, ma'am. Yes, ma'am. Just passing through on my way to save my pitiful excuse for a friend, Marie Chandler. I'll drag her back by way of the sidewalk. I will, I will. I promise." This is a lie, of course. It's okay to deceive the enemy, Daddy says. On my return trip with my scaredy-cat buddy, we just duck low, below the tops of the azaleas, and skitter across the lawn without making a sound. Flying under the radar, as Daddy always does when

Mother is on one of her ranting and raving riles. But this story was supposed to be about being scared. And, as hard as it is for this future F.B.I. agent to admit it, fear is something I've met before. At this rate you might be thinking that maybe I'm afraid of *Mrs. Brigga-ding-bat*, or that maybe I'm afraid of her yard, of all things. No, no, that couldn't be further from the facts of life. The person I'm scared of the most is really Marie Chandler's daddy, Mr. Phillip Bobby John Thompkins. Yep, they all have long names. And they call themselves by as many at one time as the air in one set of lungs can accommodate. You try saying, "Well, hello there, Mr. Phillip Bobby John Thompkins," a few times and see how winded you get. It's a wonder anyone has air left to start another sentence after spitting all that out in greeting. Maybe it does have to do with them being from Georgia and having Tara in their blood. You might be wondering by now just why I happen to be scared of Marie Chandler's Mr. Phillip Bobby John. With good reason, I suppose, since I have the tendency to be long-winded and get sidetracked when a story starts forming in the overly creative imagination my brain happens to own. The details seem to misdirect me, Mother says. "Just the facts," Daddy always prods. "Skip the details and cut to the facts, Doodlebug," he warns. Well, I'm afraid of Mr. Phillip Bobby John because of Marie Chandler's pronouncement on our way to Vacation Bible School last summer. We were just riding along, minding our own business, Mother trying to maneuver the big curves on North Mendenhall, me readjusting my pink dotted-Swiss bloomer ruffles so I'd look pretty when I climbed out of the station wagon when we arrived at The Church of the Crucifixion of Jesus. Marie Chandler had just finished telling Mother that her aunt and uncle, whose names are too long and complicated for me to rattle off here without me getting sidetracked again, were coming for a visit from Atlanta and that she was not too excited about having "relative strangers" sleeping down the hall from her for two weeks. She was staring out the window as she talked, as if nothing she had to say was of any great importance, and as if her telling about the future visitors would prove to my mother that she could carry on adult conversation like they were teaching us to do at Junior League Cotillion classes each week. I was hardly even listening because I figured Marie Chandler was "sucking up," as Daddy says all the Thompkinses were "born and bred to do." Then, Marie Chandler said, "I just hope Poppa doesn't break another door down while they are here, like he did last night." My Wrigley's DoubleMint fell, *kerplop*, right out of my mouth and into my lap. The car lurched sideways as Mother almost took out the brick mailbox and three crepe myrtles on the corner of Mendenhall and Shady Grove. She regained control of the land-yacht and managed to brake before running the red light at White Station in front of the church. Mother's voice squeezed out of her in a pitch that could shatter Hobnail glass. "Why, Marie Chandler, whatever do you mean? Why on God's green earth would your father break down a door?"—"Cause Momma made him 'hoppin' mad, that's why," Marie Chandler said, as if it were the most rational of explanations her little mind could conjure up. "Hell's bells, Marie Chandler," I almost yelled, not even caring if a good mouth-washing with Ivory liquid was in my future. "Did your Mother tell him she had a headache and needed to take two aspirin and go to bed early or something? Or did he catch her fooling around, like those soap opera women she watches on *Days of Our Lives* do everyday?"—"Amy Smith!" Mother spat. "Hush your mouth. You don't know what you are talking about." The station wagon pulled to a catawampus stop just to the left of the massive crucifix of the dying Jesus in our church's parking lot. Mother rolled up her window, in spite of the heat, reached across the empty passenger seat and cranked that window up while motioning for me to do the same. Marie Chandler rolled hers up too, so as not to be left out, I suppose. Heat vapors rose within the stale confines of the car faster than the drainage ditch behind the outhouse fills to overflowing during a spring thunderstorm. "Now, Marie Chandler," Mother began as she slung her arm over the seat. She looked sideways at me in a warning to keep my mouth shut. Her face then remolded itself into her "Yes, dear, you can confide in me," mask. "Tell me what you mean, dear. Did your Daddy really break down a door, or was it stuck because of this humidity and just needed a shoulder and a shove?"—"Oh, yes, ma'am. He broke it down all right. He and Momma had been yelling for hours. When she slammed the bedroom door and locked it, he couldn't take it no more and the hinges were no match for his strength." I had never known my mother to be speechless. Her lips started moving, but no words escaped them. She remoistened them the way she had taught me to do when I couldn't think of the answer when my teacher asked an unusually hard question. Then, without saying another thing, she turned around and rolled her window back down. "Well, then," she finally offered, "you girls have a good time at Vacation Bible School. I'll be along directly. Please tell Mrs. Ferguson that I have run to the grocery store and will return momentarily with snacks for your class." I recognized this as one of Mother's "diversionary tactics," as Daddy called them. I wasn't sure if she would get her act together and turn Marie Chandler's admission into a Sunday school lesson like she did whenever someone said something "inappropriate for little ears," or if we'd better high-tail it out of there before the "mushroom from her A-bomb" descended upon us all. I waited a few extra minutes to make sure I didn't draw attention to myself, then decided it was time for us to skee-daddle out of there. I pried the door open and dragged Marie Chandler out as quickly as I could. When Mrs. Ferguson led us in the singing of "There is a balm in Gilead that heals the sinful soul," I thought of Mr. Phillip Bobby John and hoped God would grant him that salve. That afternoon, while I handed damp laundry to Mother to hang out on the line, she announced that I was not to go over to Marie Chandler's house "until further notice." I knew in my gut that that meant never. This news saddened me more than the death of Grandmother Gaston had. Marie Chandler has never once asked me why we always have to play at my house now. I hear *Mrs. Bugger-miester* yelling and I come a-running to save my friend from the neighborly foe, wishing all the while that I could save her from Mr. Phillip Bobby John, the father that haunts my dreams and makes me wish **Simper Fi** worked for parents as easily as it works for grumpy neighbors and mistreated lawns.

# Her Virtue

The beat of my heart floats
on a rhythmic
channel of giddy exhilaration each time
I watch my daughter concentrate
on math.
The tiny
furrows around her eyes, still
moist with youth, fold into long
envelopes of understanding.
The deep
dimple above her right brow
punctuates
the serious nature of her thought.

Tonight, her pondering is
on Veritas,
its meaning to our school,
our faith,
our lives.
She writes from a perspective
of wonder,
a wide-eyed rebel learning
early on the benefits
of wisdom,

the challenge
of living
up to a virtue many folks have
discarded,
tossed to the arena where popular
opinion rules.

She grips her pen
like I do
—both defiant, we are—
The slant of her cursive wavers
from a forceful leftward lean
to a strident soldier of
righteousness.
Does she dare to speak her mind?
I think so.
She echoes what has been taught her,
only to follow up quickly with
her thoughts on the matter.
How Truth permeates her life . . .
     . . . is what counts.

# Finding the Right Church

*(Published in* Living by Faith, *Obadiah Press 2003)*

When we moved to Florida, the first thing on our agenda was to find a church home. We had never had to shop around for a church. We'd attended the same one in North Carolina for years and were perfectly happy there. So, this was a new experience for us. We had already decided that we wouldn't feel comfortable at "the beach church." You know, the church closest to the beach where all the tourists flock in their flip-flops and tastelessly disguised beach attire. That would not be the proper atmosphere in which to bring up our darling little daughter. No need to visit there, even though it was located less than a half a mile from our home.

Instead, we drove eight miles down the highway to the *other* church. And oh, what a beautiful church it is. Massive beams support dark wooden rafters, padded pews and kneelers face a formal altar with a bank of windows opening to all of God's Nature beyond. It is a magnificent place. And the perfect place, I thought. This was the church for us; I was certain. So, the next day I called the church office and registered our little darling for faith formation classes. We were set; now we just needed to get involved and meet some people to help make us feel at home, right?

I had never before realized that churches have personalities. I never knew that a building could breathe, could communicate, could speak to me, but this building did. Oh, and the parishioners we met were such lovely people, friendly and welcoming. The priest was a warm and jolly

Irishman, who had wonderful homilies and always got us out of there on time. What more could a person ask of a church, I wondered?

But something wasn't quite right. As much as I liked the building and the people in it, as much as I tried to make this church work for me, it lacked something—I just wasn't sure what. It lacked that intangible something that I couldn't grasp at first. I would sit in Mass waiting for that feeling. You know the feeling. That "ah ha" feeling you get when you know you are at home. As moving as the homilies were, as dynamic and fulfilling as Communion was, I didn't feel that spiritual connection that I had grown so accustomed to in the church we'd left behind. What could be wrong? I started to doubt my connectedness with God. Was I not participating in the Mass the way I should? Was I not "into it" the way I should be? I vowed to try harder. I would make this church work.

Then it happened.

We ran late one Sunday morning. We didn't have time to drive the eight miles from our home and get to Mass on time. What were we to do? Did we dare visit *the beach church*? It looked like we had no choice.

We piled into the car and arrived within two minutes, not knowing what to expect, but dreading it just the same. We couldn't see the church from the parking lot, and were surprised to find a labyrinth of pathways leading from all directions through a natural wooded area and intersecting at the sanctuary entrance. Statues and meditation alcoves nestled among the trees along the paths, and a large bricked area lay before the great doors leading into the foyer. I was impressed, but of course, I didn't let on. This wasn't our church. We were just visiting out of necessity.

We entered a large foyer and were greeted by a multitude of 'welcomers' and the priest himself, a forty-something ex-surfer bum wearing Birkenstocks, rimless glasses and a buzz cut. Interesting, I thought with a sneer. Six-foot tall urns in rustic shades of gold, green and copper stood sentry outside and inside the space. We passed through tall doors into the sanctuary where the slate tile floor vanished before us into a huge baptismal pool. People knelt to dip their fingers in the waters and bless themselves, or they paused at a raised font, gurgling softly and flowing down into the larger pool. Glass surrounded us on all sides, giving the sensation of a natural amphitheater surrounded by woods. Pews encircled the altar, positioned squarely at the heart of the grand circular room. I glanced up. A faceted crystal and wooden cross hung above the altar, with a kaleidoscope of light and color reflecting through it, spilling the morning sun into the room. I didn't realize I had stopped and was gawking until another astonished visitor bumped into me from behind.

We shuffled to an un-upholstered pew. I genuflected toward the center of the room, unable to decipher exactly where they had hidden the tabernacle. *Strike one,* I thought. *The tabernacle should be in full view.* I was looking for a box, a gold box with doors like the one we'd had in North Carolina, and I didn't take the time to notice the candles around what I had thought to be the altar. It was the tabernacle. They had placed Christ exactly where He should be, at the heart of the room.

We sat down, and I failed to stop myself from gazing around the space to see what else there was to see. "Not exactly my taste. Too contemporary, too cold," I whispered to my husband, unwilling to acknowledge that this place was really pretty neat.

The priest processed in, proceeded by all the Eucharistic ministers. A small choir, accompanied by stringed instruments and horns, led the congregation in the opening hymn. That's when I noticed it—no missals, no hymnals. Everyone sang along from the bulletins that the flock of welcomers had handed out when we first arrived. *Strike two,* I thought. *They are too cheap to buy missals. What will everyone do without pages upon pages of text to shuffle through during Mass?*

The priest stood beside his chair during all the readings, with his arms crossed over his chest and his chin raised like an approving (or disapproving depending on your perspective) schoolmaster overseeing his adolescent flock. Latecomers filed in, dressed in garb ranging from tacky to flat out tasteless, and most of which wouldn't be appropriate attire for a rock concert. How could anyone wear such clothes to church? *Strike three,* I thought, at which time I decided to just suck it up, suffer through it and not worry about it because we were never coming back.

That's when it happened again.

The priest began his homily. He was intelligent, funny and engaging. In spite of my negative attitude, his words reached out and grabbed me, touching on something significant that had happened to me that very week. This bothered me. I hadn't counted on feeling anything. I hadn't counted on this. *Visitors luck*, I told myself.

I glared at my watch; the priest was running long, very long. I patted my foot. *This won't do. This won't do at all. We'll see what he can do with the celebration of the Eucharist. If I don't get goosebumps, he's toast.*

How arrogant I was. I positioned myself to make it impossible for the priest or for God to get through. I closed my stance, made no eye contact, offered and gave nothing whatsoever of myself. I was determined not to like this church, or this priest. I was determined not to acknowledge the tug at my heart.

The priest lifted the host. "Take this, and eat it, this is my body, which will be given up for you."

*What's this*, I wondered? The priest held a loaf of real unleavened bread, not those pasty wafers, but real bread. I glanced around the sanctuary, counting heads. There were seven hundred people present— easy. I multiplied that by the number of Masses on a given weekend. Some angelic parishioner had been very busy making bread. I had never experienced this before.

> It's food too fine for angels;
> Yet come, take
> And eat thy fill! It's Heaven's
> Sugar cake.
>
> —Edward Taylor, *Sacramental Meditations 8*

The hairs on my arms were the first to react. A lump wiggled its way up my throat. I swallowed hard, but couldn't force it down. My eyes stung, and tears rolled. My fingers tingled and goosebumps exploded across my skin like happy poison ivy on steroids. Goosebumps!!! Blessed goosebumps. They were back in full force, oh, where had they been?

I quaked through the remainder of the celebration, riveted by every aspect and nuance. When the Mass ended, I staggered to my feet and shuffled out of the sanctuary, still reeling from a spiritual experience these words struggle and fail to express. I pushed through the massive doors leading into the outer courtyard and stopped dead as if my feet had been epoxied to the concrete.

Before me stood a huge crucifix. The most magnificent depiction of Christ's suffering and His love for us I had ever seen. How had I missed this when we first arrived? Now that I had seen it, how could I leave?

I stared up at this work of art, awestruck by its beauty, stabbed by its power and meaning. This was the place. This was the church. This was where my family was supposed to be.

Now, you may be asking yourself . . . Is this woman crazy? She chooses her church by how many goosebumps it generates? How many tears flow or how beautiful the surroundings? Well, no, not exactly, but I can't say you're all wrong. I believe that when God wants us to be somewhere, when he wants us to do something and we refuse to listen or cooperate, He uses personality specific ways to help us along. For me He uses goosebumps, and most certainly tears. My priest in Charlotte used to say that my bladder was located behind my eyeballs, and at the slightest provocation, it had a great tendency to leak.

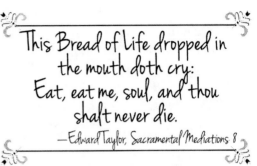

This Bread of Life dropped in the mouth doth cry: Eat, eat me, soul, and thou shalt never die.
—Edward Taylor, Sacramental Meditations 8

We all know the feeling of God's finger on our backs, the little signals He uses to help us along our path. We don't always acknowledge them, but we usually know when we're doing what's right, or when we're doing what's wrong. What I learned, once again, from my refusal to listen to God's wishes, is that He's always there for us, regardless. Even when we put up obstacles and attitudes that the most patient of family members wouldn't tolerate, God doesn't mind. God is different. His Living Water is fresh and clean and pure no matter where on our path we happen to be.

But in those wondrous moments when we feel Him, when we find that right place, or that right thing, His Water is so irresistible, so sweet. Our faith comes alive. There is no question that it is God talking. There is no possibility to shake it off, to disregard it as coincidence or luck—It is God. He is speaking directly to us. And we listened! We actually listened, but more importantly, we heard!

We now attend the beach church, and I fathom to say we always will. I'm not sure exactly why He wanted us there. It's convenient, that's nice, and we are getting involved. All I know is that when I am there I am home. Our little darling manages the long Masses without incident, which is a miracle in itself. And the vacation crowds don't affect me. Standing room only must be pleasing to God, don't you think? I look at them all as innocents who haven't a clue what they've walked in to, and I pray that God will zing them the way he did me.

Every time I enter the vestibule a little saying goes through my heart as I walk down the aisle to my seat . . .

*There's no place like home. There's no place like home. Amen.*

Author Note:

One never knows what God has in store . . .

We no longer live in Destin, where we had moved to "retire." No, we are now back home in Memphis, the city of my birth, a city to which I never dreamed I would return. We are no longer retired either. I am pleased to still declare, however, "There's no place like home!"

Amen.

# I Never Thanked You

I never thanked you

Your wish breathed me
life, all powder and wrinkles.
A new doll, I was,
diapers fastened with
duck safety pins.

I never thanked you

By two, my feet in
the sink, we teetered on the
white porcelain cusp between
friendship and sisterhood,
a realm blurred by
the vastness of thirteen long years.

I never thanked you

Curls coaxed by your patience,
smoothed 'round pink foam with
blue dabs of Dippity-Doo.
You drew me in shades
and shadows, as surely as
the artist that couldn't lift
her pencil from the page.

I never thanked you

Abandoned at ten, though,
again at sixteen and twenty-one,
the losses shifted my trajectory.
I splayed against a wind blown in
gusty spurts that rocked the
cradle of my confidence.
Slashed red shreds of me
flung to the far ends of my
world, only to be gathered up
by you, swept back into the
semblance of someone else's smile.

I never thanked you

I shouldered my own
desertions by failing,
but learned to float by your
example as your sorrow
reflected blue in the
china patterns and Chinese
warriors upon your wall.

(Continued on next page)

# I Never Thanked You (continued)

I counted your teardrops in
the crystal figures that
lined the glass shelves of
your curio, blown
darners awaiting mending
that never got done.

I never thanked you

Your inaudible mantra of
forging ahead led the
way to sun washed days,

fostered by memory rich
with cinnamon, sugar and pecans.
Though antiquities bond us,
ancient losses lay healed,
freshly cleansed by
the palpable understanding
of your wishing breath.

I never thanked you

Thank you

# *Braised Goat's Head with Sadza and Tripe*

Adding a dash of something unexpected to a culinary concoction can elevate a recipe from mundane to magnificent. Apricot Liqueur in Sissie's Fruitcake Cookies is the perfect example of this, or Mother's addition of fresh coconut milk to her white cake batter, or Sissie's recent discovery that "Mickel's Pickles" brand transforms tuna salad into something quite unique. It works the same way in life. As I wrote in my preface, the people you've read about in this collection, both the flesh-n-blood varieties and the fictional ones that exist only in my head, are the unexpected and blessed ingredients that have spiced the recipe of my life. They may not make much sense when scattered about in stories, but when mixed together just so-so and allowed to simmer awhile, their richness melds and marries the life experiences of the most divine recipe in the universe: my life.

(I'll take this uncommon opportunity to thank them all for their contributions to the making of me. I love you and would not be me without you.)

But just when I thought I had learned a thing or ten about life, that I'd reached some level of wisdom to elevate me above any slimy okra that might be tossed into my mix, God shook me up with something radical and a plot so thick with miracles this fiction writer could never have imagined it on even my most creative of days.

I arrived at the Panera Bread Company in Germantown, Tennessee at 11 a.m. sharp, a full thirty minutes early for my meeting with Dan Nisser of the Cargill Company. Kathy Boccia, my boss, had agreed to join us. She and I had been knocking around ideas for the past several months, but I wasn't sure anything would come of the discussions. We hoped to find ways to include more 21st Century teaching techniques into the curriculum at St. Agnes Academy-St. Dominic School, and that might mean introducing our students to a different kind of education, one that involved commitment and caring, one that involved reaching beyond ourselves to make a difference in a world beyond the boundaries of Memphis, Tennessee.

As I stood in line, pondering the expensive coffee options before me, I couldn't wrestle my thoughts away from the obvious question: How had I, a middle-aged Southern mother, gotten myself mixed up in a scheme with such long-distance possibilities? I had a hard enough time maneuvering the educational and social landscapes right here at home. Could I handle this challenge? And if I already doubted myself, what hope would I have of success?

I groaned to myself and paid an exorbitant $4.50 for a fancy cup of coffee with a three-inch tall stack of whipped cream atop the steaming caffeine surge. I resisted the Cinnamon Crunch Bagel, but regretted the decision as soon as I sat down next to a woman who had lost her battle to be good and was enjoying the exact delicacy.

I groaned again. Was my life just a series of food choices? Every event seemed punctuated by culinary sensations, both savory and sweet. I decided to live vicariously through the woman's choice and inhaled deeply, imagining myself biting into the crusty pastry, the honey walnut cream cheese oozing from the sides of my mouth.

Dietary torture it was, I tell you, torture in its purest and most horrific form. To divert my misery, I allowed my thoughts to wander back to the previous spring. It had all begun in class one day while discussing with my students what it means to be a "global citizen." They challenged my philosophy that all humanity is linked by the joys and struggles of our human experience. A simple hypothesis, I thought. But they got downright confrontational when I explained that the harsh edges of our differences blur and realign themselves into the clarity of understanding when we share our life stories with each other and become friends. It was wonderful enough that my students questioned me, exhilarating in fact, but what happened next, and after that, and after that, has been miraculous. I have to remind myself often to take it one breath at a time.

"Do you really believe that just *getting to know someone* can change the world, Mrs. Schuster?" one young man had asked. "You think that just hanging out and telling a few jokes or stories can demolish prejudice and knock down social, economic and religious barriers that have kept people at odds for centuries?" He was one of my brighter 7th grade students, full of himself and his advanced vocabulary. He chuckled, and coughed out a hearty, "Yeah, right."

I nodded. "Yes, that's what I really believe. If we can keep people from talking about politics and religion long enough, and focus them first on revealing themselves, sharing their lives, who they are as individuals, as fathers or mothers, sisters, brothers, friends, get them talking about the traditions and celebrations that are important to them, about who they love, why they love, what struggles challenge them the most, how they name their children, what recipes they serve at birthdays and weddings, at wakes and funerals, what traditions have been handed down from one generation to the next—if we can do that, then yes, the world will change for the better right before our eyes—one person at a time, until we're all friends."

But no, this bunch of students wasn't so easy to convince. They wanted proof. They wanted to test my theory and reach out to people on the other side of the world, people they knew nothing about and with whom they believed they had little in common. I should have realized it then. When students get interested enough in an idea to want to *do* something about it, the teacher better hang on and be ready for a wild ride. Enthusiastic students cannot be bridled or subdued; they mean business and want answers. Engaged students are creator gods that force teachers to be great. Where do you think the world gets great teachers in the first place? They are created in classrooms everywhere, classrooms armed with students who have the guts to raise their hands and say, "Hey, I don't think you're right about that." They wrestle teachers out of the way so they can get down to the important business of changing the world.

Phew! Even the memory made me breathless.

The lady with the bagel beside me moaned with delight and I was catapulted back to the present. I checked my watch—11:15. Why was I early for everything? Even when I try to be late, I fail miserably, giving myself too much time to think. Thankfully, Dan showed up a few minutes after I'd completed my first cup of Joe and was considering the disadvantages of another. He extended his hand in greeting.

"What you spent on that coffee could pay a whole term's tuition at a school in Zimbabwe, you know," he said, pulling up a chair. My desire for that second cup vaporized with a sudden gust of guilt. "If you're interested in connecting with people in a developing nation, your idea of normal will have to be checked at the door."

I resisted the urge to defend myself by telling him that I had not bought a bagel.

Kathy arrived about that time and Dan shared several examples of the circumstantial and cultural experiences he'd survived during his own global education with Cargill.

"A few months ago, the wife of one of our employees in Zimbabwe went into labor, but while he was driving her to the hospital, his car blew a tire," Dan began. "Another employee happened by and offered to help, but keep in mind, they were in the African bush miles from the nearest hospital and the wife's labor pains were severe. The two men managed to jack up the car, but inches below the ground where they stood high voltage electric lines had been haphazardly stretched across the road and lay hidden just under the dirt."

I gripped my mug, anticipating the tragic ending that was sure to come.

"The shock cooked the husband's body from the inside out," Dan told us, "but he miraculously survived the initial shock. The Good Samaritan ended up delivering the baby in the backseat of the car, managed to get some help, and somehow got the man to a one-room clinic nearby. One look and the doctors knew they could do little to help."

Dan paused, a gray pallor now shadowing his face, then continued, talking to the table

> The Lord measures our perfection neither by the multitude nor the magnitude of our deeds, but by the manner in which we perform them.
> —St John of the Cross

now. "Since he was a Cargill employee, I was contacted about what to do. They called *me*, here in Memphis, from Zimbabwe, wanting to know if they should let the man die or try to get him to a hospital many miles away. Even under the best circumstances, his chances were slim, but a man's life was at stake. No one could have prepared me for this kind of decision, but that's how it is in third world countries. The simple, everyday people have no one to help them."

Dan explained that airlifting the man to the closest burn unit in South Africa would have taken too much time; the man wouldn't have survived the flight or the wait. They had to think more creatively. They needed a medical staff and a place that could be quickly sterilized, so Dan authorized the *purchase* of the nearest hospital, which was no more than an ill-equipped clinic run by Doctors Without Borders.

"The doctors turned the clinic into a make-shift burn unit and nursed the man for 16 days."

This pause in the story only added to my distress. I knew what was coming and shored myself up for the blow.

"On day 17, he died from an infection caused by lack of supplies and the inability to keep the place properly sterilized. It is hard for us to imagine, but people all over the world face challenges like this every day. When I took this job," Dan said, visibly shaken from his emotional recitation, "I never imagined a life or death decision like this would ever be left up to me."

I, too, was having trouble wrapping my mind around it all. I felt nauseous as sorrow churned the hazelnut liquid in my stomach that had seemed so appealing just moments before. One look Kathy's way let me know that she felt the same way. Her fresh napkin now lay in shreds around the base of her untouched coffee cup.

Dan told story after story and my enthusiasm about offering my students a "global education" rose and waned, depending on the outcome of each tale. By the end of our discussion I wondered if I could handle this new mission. Could a white woman from Memphis, Tennessee process the realities this world had to offer? More important, could I introduce junior high students to those realities? It all seemed too much. I'd been insulated for so long from the world's abject poverty and blatant disregard for human life and human rights. The poorest of the poor in the United States are wealthy in comparison to so many millions in other parts of the world. At least our poor have government programs to help them. Most developing nations offer nothing to their poor. Suddenly, our excitement about making a "global connection" seemed naïve and self-serving. What had we expected? A happy story about how easy it would be to introduce our students to our beautiful world?

Dan let the gravity of his stories settle upon us for a few moments. Smart man—he realized that Kathy and I were too overcome to speak and needed time to adjust. Finally, the crack of his fist hitting the table jarred us out of our despondence. "I didn't tell you this to dissuade you," he almost shouted, his words forcing us to look him in the eye. "Quite the contrary. My question to you is: Will you help? And don't say yes, unless you recognize that this is a marathon, not a sprint. You've got to commit for the long haul and realize that this will be the most rewarding thing you can do for yourselves and for your students. If you don't understand that, you might as well get up and go back to teaching from a book."

The ring shook me awake. I stumbled into the kitchen, but the call had already rolled over to voicemail before I could pick it up. The number was unfamiliar, and since I was still sleep-dazed and about to wet my pants, I plodded back to bed, after a quick pit stop, only to reawaken, stock-stiff and wide-eyed, moments later. "Could that have been Dan?" I whispered to no one. I slipped from beneath the covers, shrugged into my robe and headed for the phone.

His voicemail was short and to the point. "I'll call you back at 5 o'clock your time. Hope you answer. The headmistress of the Saruwe Junior School wants to talk to you."

A rush of adrenaline chased away any residual slumber. I placed my phone on the table in front of me and stared at it, then almost jumped out of the chair when it rang at 5 a.m.

"Hello, Dan?" The air crackled with static, as if dragging his words through gravel as they made their way across the world to me.

"I'm in Selous, Zimbabwe. I have much to share, but first, I'd like for you to speak with Headmistress Eunice Sengayi. She is very excited about the possibilities we discussed."

My tiny cell phone was now perched on my open palm, as if it had morphed into a consecrated Host eagerly waiting to renew my life. I don't say this to be disrespectful, but I view the responsibility we've accepted as a sacred gift, one that requires all the reverence and dedication we can give it. I was humbled by the magnitude of this phone call, as humbled as I am each time I walk the Communion aisle to receive my Lord. This miracle of connecting with the Saruwe School had become a personal sign sent from heaven, a signal that this crazy scheme was, in fact, a divine mission God had planned all along. I did not know why Kathy and I been chosen, but I wanted the choosing to be God's idea and not my own ego directing Him to do what I desired. This was *my* dream, wasn't it? Now, I wanted to know if it could be my dream and God's plan, too.

"Helllllluuuuu? Mrs. Schuuuuuster? Are you there?"

Mrs. Sengayi's voice was high-pitched and earthy, as if the mysterious cadence of tribal drums in the distance lived within it and was only tempered by the proper lilt of a grand British lady at high tea.

"Yes, yes, I'm here. It is so nice to finally speak with you. Please tell me about yourself and your school."

She introduced herself simply and then related the specifics about her school. Six hundred and fifty students, grades K-8, no electricity, no running water, no desks, twelve classrooms, twenty teachers, no supplies, no textbooks, one hundred children crammed into a classroom on rainy days, classes that meet outside on days when the temperature allows it and the season is dry.

She seemed embarrassed in the telling, as if sharing these intimate details of their lacking was some sort of betrayal on her part, that revealing their dire circumstances might focus an unpleasant light on her school and its students and let them down in some way. Her words rushed at me over the phone lines in short bursts of honesty, then paused, hesitant and halting. Her meekness touched me on a visceral level. I sensed her devotion to her students and her desperation to do whatever it took to make life better for them, even if it meant begging an American teacher for help.

Of course, we wanted to help, but as her list of needs grew longer,

I wondered if the challenge was already too immense. Did we really want to *adopt* almost seven hundred pupils and twenty teachers and take on the responsibility for their need? Notice that my pronouns have now shifted to the "multi-plural" form, if there is such a thing. This was no longer *my vision, my desire, my dream*. No, it wasn't even the "little we" visions of only Kathy and me. The two of us couldn't handle this alone. Sure, Kathy's backing and encouragement were wonderful, but this was bigger than us. It had to be a big *We* project, a school-supported project. *We* needed reassurance that St. Agnes Academy-St. Dominic School and its administration would back us up. After listening to Mrs. Sengayi's plea, I had to wonder if *we* had already created a challenge of which failure could be our only response.

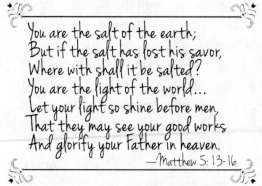

You are the salt of the earth;
But if the salt has lost his savor,
Where with shall it be salted?
You are the light of the world...
Let your light so shine before men,
That they may see your good works
And glorify your Father in heaven.
—Matthew 5: 13-16

"Yes, yes, Mrs. Sengayi," I muttered, "I'm taking notes. I understand. I will talk to my dean and the president of our school and we will be back in touch with you. There is much to consider. I appreciate your time."

"Oh, God, bless you, Mrs. Schuster," she said before hanging up the phone. "You are an angel sent by God to my students. We are so blessed that Mr. Dan came to visit us today. Good-bye for now."

My hand came to rest in my lap, a new kind of exhaustion adding heaviness to my spirit. Responsibility is much heavier than love. I looked up. My daughter was standing in the doorway.

"Was that Mr. Dan and the school in Africa?" she asked. "Are we going to help them, Mom? That would be so cool."

I smiled, refreshed by her exuberance. Cool, yes. My own daughter was one of those students I mentioned earlier, the ones that leap upon opportunity, grab it just behind the earlobes and ride it like a wild bull, expecting all the while that they will survive the bucking, subdue the beast and land safely on their feet. Our new Global Ambassadors Board at school had already planned and hosted a fundraiser for the Saruwe School. They'd sold chicken biscuits and tasty Panera bagels for breakfast before school each week and hosted a used book sale, with a huge yard sale planned for early spring. They'd written pen pal letters to Saruwe students and shared stories about their lives. They were ready for action and already frustrated that all they'd gotten so far was talk.

"Yes, honey. We're going to help them," I said with a sigh. "I'm not sure how, but we're going to do our very best. I think that's what God wants us to do."

Miracles dropped hard and fast after that. My ambitious Global Ambassadors leaped into more action. They created a web site and researched the social justice issues affecting our world. They studied the United Nation's Millennium Development Goals and made videos to teach others about ways to make our world a better place. I held on to the Holy Spirit's coattails as He dragged me along, never knowing what He might do next to convince me that we were on the right track.

Yet another phone call awakened me, this one at 10 o'clock one evening in December. The voice of Gretchen Kirk, a friend from work who is also our Director of Religious Education, jolted me from near slumber. "Oh, Julia, are you sitting down? You won't believe this. You just won't believe what's happened now!"

"I'm actually in bed. What time is it?" I fumbled for the clock.

"Doesn't matter. Wake up! You won't believe it, I tell you. Wake up."

Gretchen and Kathy were attending a Christmas party at St. Peter's, a local church.

"A tall black man was standing all alone at the back of the room," Gretchen explained, "looking like he'd been dropped from another planet and had no idea where he was. Well, I had to go and say hello. He looked so lost, so alone."

Kathy's voice chimed in from somewhere close by. "Gretchen felt drawn to him. You know how she is." Her voice got louder as she wrestled for the phone. "She made a bee-line over to him. That Southern hospitality, you know. Her mother raised her well."

"The man said he was from South Africa! Can you believe it? I almost screamed," Gretchen exclaimed, ripping the phone back from Kathy's hands. "Can you believe it? He had been to Dallas to visit his sister and stopped off in Memphis so he could visit the St. Martin de Porres Shrine. That's the reason he *thinks* he is here, Julia, but I told him that God sent him to us, and that God was using him for something wonderful. The poor man thought I was crazy, I'm sure."

Kathy grumbled in the background, "You are. We all know that," followed by a hearty laugh.

Gretchen had formally accosted Fr. Lewis Tsuro with a rapid-fire explanation about our "African Mission" and had told him about our desire to connect with other schools in the region. She explained that Kathy and I had been invited to visit the Saruwe School in Zimbabwe in February, but that the trip seemed impossible because we'd have to lay over in Johannesburg for several days while Dan took care of other business. "Two women alone in Johannesburg won't do," she'd explained to the shell-shocked minister. "They need someone to watch over them. Don't you see? God sent you to us, Fr. Lewis. And you thought you just came to Memphis to visit a shrine."

By this point in the conversation, I was glad Gretchen had warned me to be seated because I was on my feet, pacing back and forth beside the bed and feeling like I might faint. I reached for the bed for support, while babbling over and over, "You must be joking! Oh, Gretchen. I have goosebumps the size of Montana on my arms."

"You haven't heard it all, Julia. He's a teacher! He teaches religion at a Catholic school, and you'll never guess the name of it: It's *Veritas*, Julia. He teaches at Veritas College, a K-12 Catholic school outside of Johannesburg, just like our school's motto, *Veritas*. Can you believe it? God delivered Fr. Lewis from Johannesburg and he is coming to meet you tomorrow! He can't wait for you to come to Africa and visit his school!"

God is good all the time, and all the time, God is good.

A few weeks later my husband, Peter and I celebrated our 27th anniversary. I gave him a leaf blower, of all things, justifying that it was his favorite outdoor tool and that he needed a new one. (Lame, I know, but I actually believe he gets some kind of pleasure out of blowing leaves and tidying up our "bunker," as he calls home.) He gave me a watch.

To most people, a watch is a fairly normal anniversary gift, nothing unique or special, but for us, from Peter, for me especially, it was monumental and very symbolic. You see, I have never worn a watch. They always felt constrictive on my wrist and, quite frankly, I didn't like seeing all those minutes fly by. Time passes too quickly as it is. I didn't appreciate the visual image of the second hand's race around the face every 60 seconds. But when I opened Peter's gift, the connections and underlying meanings of it flooded over me and I couldn't speak. He had said so often that this was "my time." He had commented that my confidence had blossomed and I was finally figuring out my "true calling." Until that moment and in light of all the wonders that had dragged me to that point, I hadn't understood what he meant. I realized then that my true calling is to teach—myself, my family and my students—that we have a responsibility to this world. My mission is to teach and to write about anything and everything I figure out along the way because real education is hidden in the deciphering process.

I have been married to this man for more than half of my life. He has been so patient with me. He has held my hand, caught my tears, nudged my back and applauded my successes for longer than my own parents had the opportunity to do. He knows me better than I know myself. His gift of time has been more generous and loving than I ever deserved. On that day of our anniversary, I looked at that beautiful watch and I saw our commitment, our faith, our love for each other. Peter didn't think I liked it. He didn't think I *got it*. And I didn't have the words to explain to him just how deeply the simple gift of a watch meant to me.

Admitting that I didn't (and still don't) have the words was a miracle in itself. As hard as I had tried to put words to my life, as desperately as I had worked to make sense of it all, to analyze the mystery of God by forcing words upon it, I still learn daily that some things cannot be explained. My love for my husband is one of those things. Another is explaining God's work in my life, how He forms me and leads me and is present in everything I do, even when I try to shut Him out. He is certainly working through me with this Global Ambassadors/African Mission thing. My words will never do Him justice, but I will keep right on plugging away, tapping my thoughts into words, sentences and paragraphs. Words onto paper may never reveal God to anyone, but reading and rereading my reflections deepens my faith, and I think that's what it's all about.

At 7:42 p.m. the tires of Delta Flight 200 to Johannesburg lifted-off from Atlanta, and with them, my spirit. Kathy and I were on our way. We sat in seats 36F and G, across the aisle from each other. The evening sun had already disappeared and darkness enveloped the great aircraft as we powered toward a new world. Dan and another company employee, ex-FBI agent Steve, sat several rows in front of us in business first class. The 18 hours it would take before we touched down in "Jo'burg" seemed insignificant in the grand scheme of events that had brought us to this point.

Seven mammoth bags of school supplies and sports equipment, all collected and packed by my beloved students, rested below us in the belly of the plane. Kathy reached across the aisle and squeezed my hand. I was too excited to be nervous.

Three days later, I was seated at a small table on a rough wooden deck. Iwamanzi Gorge is dark at 4 a.m., but the outline of the towering ridge across the river stood backlit with a blanket of stars so close, so luminous, I wondered if my extended fingers might disturb their slumber and knock them from their ethereal place, rolling them like shiny marbles from the sky into my awaiting lap. I had no sense of direction. I stared out into the vastness, wondering from which side of the gorge the first hints of morning's light would come. I'd never seen night so startling, never felt the vacuum of nature close around me with such intimacy. The titillating sensation kept me off balance, awake with anticipation all night.

Kathy slept in the bush room behind me. I wondered if her rest had been affected by this place. We were the only guests at Iwamanzi. We'd traveled there for a few days rest after visiting Fr. Lewis in Johannesburg and before traveling on to Zimbabwe with Dan. I was happy for the break. Twenty hours on a plane, then a three-day whirlwind tour through Johannesburg and its tumultuous history had drained me. No college course on Colonial and Contemporary African History could have taught me more. And the food, oh, the food! I could write a whole book about the delicacies, (and gastronomically disastrous) recipes we *experienced.* I had assured Fr. Lewis that I was thrilled he'd chosen the priesthood, but a successful career as a travel guide could have been an alternate choice.

I felt guilty, at first, about taking this photographic safari side trip to Iwamanzi in the Northwest Province, but now realized that God gave us this gift of rest so we could prepare ourselves for what lay ahead.

The lodge manager, Roche, and his wife, Ansu, had bid us goodnight at 8 with the warning that the generator would be turned off at 8:15. We had rushed to get ready for bed, drawing heavy curtains across the windows and mosquito nets around our beds, fearful that some foreign insect might visit us in the night and deliver an unknown virus into our bloodstreams. We'd perched in our beds, waiting, counting the seconds until darkness plunged us into the claustrophobic abyss. It took only moments of total blindness to convince us that we'd take our chances with insects in order to have what little light the night sky might grant. I'd fumbled through the blackness to draw open the curtains and my breath had caught in my chest as the radiance of African night illuminated our room.

*How many hours ago has that been,* I wondered now. *Eight? Yes, eight. I've enjoyed eight full hours of tranquility and realize only now that they are the first hours of pure serenity I've ever experienced in my life.*

I wanted to write, but was afraid. What words could I find to express this place, this peace? My laptop peeped open and its unnatural reality obliterated the night sky. Gone. Vanished. The stars retreated

> Those who trust in Him will
> understand truth,
> And the faithful will abide with
> Him in love,
> Because grace and mercy are
> upon His elect,
> And He watches over His holy ones.
>
> —Wisdom 3:9

into their black backdrop as if the invasion of artificial light into their realm was a warmonger sent to pillage and rape their celestial world. I slammed my laptop shut, seeking forgiveness for my sin and wondering if I'd broken some prehistoric law by allowing the vulgarity of technology into this sacred space.

> *God, dish it out. I can handle whatever you throw my way!*

The stars reappeared and I was ready.

Now, I fast-forward to the next week and the scene that has played in corridors of my memory every day since:

A small child stands before me, black eyes devoid of color or shadow gazing up at me as if searching to see if I have teeth in my head or if hairs have sprouted unexpectedly from my chin. Her pupils fill the spaces between her thick lashes, dark orbs that open her tiny soul to reveal innocence unspoiled. I don't know her name, or what to say to her. All I can do is smile. I try to look away, to focus on the hundreds of other children that are gathering on the school grounds, but her eyes will not let go of me. I am held captive and do not want to be freed.

Noise fills the space between us as Zimbabwean Cargill employees and Saruwe teachers move closer to the pavilion under which the dedication ceremony will be held. I look around quickly, but my gaze returns to the little girl beside me over and over again. Parents sit on rows of stone seating in the hot sun, waiting, fanning themselves with cardboard fans like my mother used years ago on hot Sundays at church in the American South. Everyone is dressed up for this occasion; women in long dresses wrapped lovingly around generous hips, men in sleeved shirts with ties that fall to mid-chest.

Close to the whitewashed buildings, a line of older students, decked out in colorful costumes, nervously prepare for their parts in the program. As they rehearse their dance steps in their minds, their hands flutter like ancient butterflies in abbreviated movement, their feet shuffle in abbreviated steps, pounding the red earth with a tribal rhythm only they can hear. Zimbabwean dignitaries also gather, brought here to "accept the handover" of the new classroom block and to get their pictures taken by the media. They greet Kathy and I with limp handshakes and stale faces. I wonder why they bothered to come. Cargill volunteers had donated the money for the new building. No Zimbabwean government funds had been used. But I am unconcerned by their intrusion. The little girl beside me holds me in her visual grasp.

Finally, I lift my camera and whisper to her, "Do you mind?" I read her slow blink as a *yes*. Her expression seems frozen, as if examining my face is the most important thing she has ever done. She is consumed with me, mesmerized. My shutter clicks and I worry that my tremulous hand has ruined the picture. The little girl does not smile or move. I cannot look away.

"Julia, Julia, Mrs. Sengayi is coming," Kathy says, tugging my sleeve. I turn and hear Eunice's lilting voice before I see her. I glance back quickly at the child. She is still watching me. I wink at her and wave as I am pulled away.

Eunice Sengayi moves through the crowd of parents and guests, parting the mass like a gentle and embracing wave, as if she has been dropped into their midst only to gather them in and welcome them to her pond. Her energy spreads out ahead of her, surrounding those around her and drawing them closer, even as they part to allow her access along her way. Kathy and I are the only white-skinned women in attendance; it isn't difficult to pick us out of the crowd. When Eunice sees

> *Christ does not force our will, He only takes what we give Him. But He does not give Himself entirely until He sees that we yield ourselves entirely to Him.*
> —St. Teresa of Avila

us, her cry rings out like a mother wolf reunited with lost cubs. We are drawn to each other like lost relations, opposite polls tugging through the vacuum of separate histories to be joined at last. Her embrace is a sacred blessing. Our tears mingle, already accustom. This is friendship at its most basic level; we know, we already know.

Then, ever so lightly, I sense a tug on my sleeve. The little girl's hand folds into mine. Eunice takes my other. And we walk the dirt pathway together to meet the Saruwe students and teachers that have captured my heart.

# Braised Goat's Head, Sadza & Tripe Recipes

1 washed and dehaired goat's head
1 huge pan
1 huge stove
1 onion and any other seasonings you might have on hand


Boil head until skin and meat pull away from skull. Hair and brains must be removed before cooking. Then, roast or braise whole head in oven until lips pull so far away from the teeth that it looks like its grinning at you and the tongue is firm to the touch. About 4 hours in a 450-degree oven, or all day over an open fire.


<u>Side note</u>: Okay, honestly, I have no idea how to braise or roast a goat's head, but Mrs. Albertine Mawela of the Johannesburg Township called "White City" knows how. She welcomed Kathy and I into her home and fed us a feast fit for an African chief. Fr. Lewis displayed great theatrical charm when he lifted the top off the bowl at the table's heart, revealing the African staple to his startled American guests. Beside the great beast were heaping bowls of mille meal or Pap—called Sadza in Zimbabwe—a thick clump of a portage-like substance made with ground maize. The tripe, well, I won't even go there, except to say that the image of Kathy's face at the moment she realized that tripe is <u>not</u> fish stew will remain emblazoned on my memory forever.

# Epilogue

Saruwe

a heart moans in
distant jacaranda arms
that weep lavender tears
only I seem to see
i turn my face to
an unknown sun and
whisper greetings in
an unknown tongue
"Mhoroyi."
i will come to you
and listen, cupping my
hands around your tales
i will knit our songs
into a new hymn
and lift it to the wind
for fresh ears
"Toonana.
Mwari Akukomborere."
God Bless.

# Acknowledgements

*The Ingredients of Gumbo* is a love letter to the people that have led me, walked with me, reeled me in and dragged me to this particular point in my life. First, I pray that every reader feels my gratitude to God for this incredible journey. He has blessed me in so many ways, most importantly with a family that teaches me daily to learn from every experience and to reach for the stars that are inscribed with my name. I never dreamed there would be so many to choose from or that it would be so fulfilling to pluck them from the sky.

Thanking my sister, Charline Shackelford, again here might be redundant, but what the heck! Sometimes there aren't enough words or opportunities. She prayed me into existence and loved me when I didn't love myself. I will forever ponder and be grateful for the mystery of sisterhood. (I love you, Sissie.) My husband, Peter, is the cornerstone onto which I have constructed so many dreams. Our life together has been graced by almost 30 years of miracles where "Let me count the ways," would take another lifetime to list. These *blaue augen* blink only for him. My personal dreams, however, owned no direction or shape until the ocean blues of our sweet Mary Kate's eyes met mine. The depth, oh, the depth I have found there, the joy and gratitude, the wonder and awe. When it comes to motherhood, all expression escapes me; there are no words, just love, just grace.

To some people, it might seem strange or even opportunistic to thank their employer publicly for the blessing of having a particular job, but those people have never worked at St. Agnes Academy-St. Dominic

School in Memphis, Tennessee. SAA-SDS is an exceptional, faith-driven family that is anchored in the Dominican charisms of Prayer, Study, Community and Service. The school is led by visionary administrators and filled with teachers that were placed upon this earth with a passion and willingness to pass on their gifts of knowledge, faith and creativity to others. What a great gift it is to enjoy daily inspiration from this cohort of enthusiastic and supportive colleagues. President Barbara Daush, the Board of Directors, the upper school dean, Joy Maness, and the St. Dominic School dean, John Murphy, deserve special thanks for their leadership. (And John for his special brand of humor that puts everything in his unique "Murphy Perspective.") I am a better teacher because of them.

As you probably deduced from my last short story, St. Agnes' lower school dean, Kathleen Toes-Boccia, and I have spent some rather adventurous times together, times that have taught me things about myself and life that fifty-three years had failed to impart. I am honored by her trust and cherish the experiences we share. This woman is dedicated, fearless and deeply spiritual. She leads by example and blesses others with her innate sense of justice and compassion. I am thankful for her leadership, friendship, council and courage, and eager to discover what our next adventure will be.

I also thank Gretchen Kirk, Pam Renfrow, Becky Hobson and every member of the SAA-SDS faculty and staff. They share their gifts so generously and effect positive change on everyone they meet. And my students . . . oh, don't get me started; I could go on for days. God is truly present in this place.

I appreciate Dan Nisser for helping Kathy and me make the connection with the Saruwe Junior School, and Priscilla Mutembwa of the Cargill Company for her friendship and continued support of our efforts to make lasting friendships in her beloved country of Zimbabwe. Father Lewis Tsuro in Johannesburg, South Africa, and his brother, Innocent, deserve special thanks for their willingness to befriend and teach a couple of clueless American women. The beauty and struggle of Africa shone through them as they unwittingly took on the challenge of becoming our tour guides. And Saruwe, oh, Saruwe! I am privileged to have developed such a close personal relationship with headmistress Eunice Sengayi. Her dedication to and compassion for her teachers and students is a testament to her gentle spirit and compassion for others. I look forward to the morsels of wisdom she will share with me next.

I cannot say enough about my sweet Judy Vermaelen, the best friend in the world (not to mention the best cook). She is my polar opposite in so many ways, but our heart songs resonate together in perfect pitch. Over the past 25 years, Judy has shared her life and family, her faith and wisdom, her friendship and council. She also lent her last name to my title story and her fabulous gumbo recipe to this collection. Yum! Could there be a better friend than that?

Finally, publishers come in all shapes and sizes, but not all publishers are created equal. After a manuscript is accepted for publication, most authors have little creative say in the rest of the process. But not so with my editors, Deborah Smith and Debra Dixon. When I sheepishly asked, "Can we make this book unique? Make it a *beautiful* book with sketches and doodles and recipes and poetry?" I was met with encouragement and a lively creative dialogue that evolved into this beautiful collection. My vision faced many challenges, but finally took physical shape in the talented hands of book designer, Martha Crockett, who lovingly gathered up the written and doodled threads and the random thoughts and ramblings I tossed her way and knit them seamlessly into the literary fabric this book has become. I had so much fun working on all the "extras" and couldn't be more pleased with the results. Thanks everyone! I love you all.

God bless!

CPSIA information can be obtained at www.ICGtesting.com
Printed in the USA
LVOW082055140512

281155LV00006B/1/P